"You think I want you, Giles?"

Leonie asked the question calmly, her lids lowered to cover her blazing blue eyes.

He gave a husky laugh. "I know you do."

"And do you want me?" she persisted.

His amusement instantly faded. "You know I do," he answered, his voice rough with desire. "You have to come to London. I can't keep seeing you here. Besides, we don't exactly have...privacy. My aunt seems to think it's the romance of the century, instead of which it's just—"

"What happens in London?" she interrupted. "The apartment, the car, the allowance?"

Giles's mouth tightened. "If that's what you want."

She took a deep breath. "No, Giles, I want more. I want *marriage*!"

His eyes widened incredulously. "You expect me to *marry* you?"

CAROLE MORTIMER
is also the author of these

Harlequin Presents

Many of these titles are available at your local bookseller.

For a free catalogue listing all available Harlequin Romances
and Harlequin Presents, send your name and address to:

HARLEQUIN READER SERVICE
1440 South Priest Drive, Tempe, AZ 85281
Canadian address: Stratford, Ontario N5A 6W2

CAROLE MORTIMER

love's duel

Harlequin Books

TORONTO • LONDON • LOS ANGELES • AMSTERDAM
SYDNEY • HAMBURG • PARIS • STOCKHOLM • ATHENS • TOKYO

For
John and Matthew

———————————————————

Harlequin Presents edition published June 1982
ISBN 0-373-10510-X

Original hardcover edition published in 1982
by Mills & Boon Limited

CHAPTER ONE

LEONIE looked up as her friend and associate came excitedly into the room, waving a letter about under her nose. 'Have you won the pools?' she teased the older woman.

'Better than that,' Emily Dryer said ecstatically. 'Giles is coming down for the weekend!'

Giles was Emily's nephew, Leonie knew that. He was senior partner in one of the most exclusive law firms in London, the pride of his doting aunt, and Leonie had heard much of him during her three months of doing the sketches for the short stories for children that Emily wrote. The two of them had met through Emily's agent; Emily was capable of writing for children but not of illustrating the stories. Despite their forty years' difference in ages, Leonie being twenty-two and Emily in her sixties, the two women managed to work very well together.

The nephew Giles had been talked about a lot, his virtues outlined for Leonie to enthuse over. He did sound a remarkable man, very young to be the senior partner of a six lawyer firm, their clients some of the most important people in the country. And according to Emily her nephew was much in demand by the ladies, apparently still being a bachelor.

'He has no use for women,' Emily had tutted after telling her this.

'None?' Leonie teased.

'I won't let you embarrass me,' Emily had fluttered. 'I'm sure Giles has his—friends, but never anything serious. There's never been anyone he thought enough of to introduce to *me*.'

From what Leonie could gather aunt and nephew were very close, so it was feasible to assume that nephew Giles had indeed never found a woman to meet his high standards. Leonie thought he sounded like a supercilious snob, but she would never let Emily know that. Dear Emily, who had treated her like the daughter she had never had. Emily seemed to make a habit of taking people's children under her wing, taking care of her nephew when her sister had disappeared from his life, and now Leonie was receiving the same care.

'She was a flighty piece,' Emily spoke of her sister. 'She should never have married a barrister. John was much too staid for her.'

From what Leonie could gather from that nephew Giles had been deprived of his mother at an early age. Maybe that accounted for his seemingly solitary existence, his way of finding women an unnecessary encumbrance. Whatever his reason, he didn't sound a very pleasant individual.

Consequently Leonie had taken a dislike to Emily's nephew before she had even met him. His profession had been enough to cause her initial dislike, and Emily's frequent assertions of what a talented barrister he was had intensified those first feelings. Leonie hated lawyers of any kind, hated their way of seeming to be on your side, and then suddenly pouncing on you. She particularly disliked one J. G. Noble, his chilling grey eyes cutting into her like a knife as he reduced her to the level of a common thief preying upon other people's weaknesses.

But she wouldn't think of that hateful man, suppressing the shiver of revulsion that rose within her just at the thought of him. She had managed to keep him out of her mind for several weeks now, the nights of waking up in a cold sweat as he called her 'nothing but a leech, a leech that should be removed from all decent society', almost becoming a thing of the past.

But she couldn't blame Emily's nephew for that, and Emily did look so excited about this surprise visit. Leonie would try to be pleasant about him, if only for Emily's sake.

'So nice of him to spare the time to visit his old aunt,' Emily chattered on. 'He's such a busy man.'

Too busy, apparently, to even visit the woman who had been a mother to him since he was five years old. 'Lawyers often are,' Leonie said noncommittally.

'Especially successful ones. Oh, Leonora, it's going to be so nice having him home again!'

Emily was the only one ever to call her Leonora, claiming from their first meeting that it was much too pretty a name to shorten in that way. Leonie didn't mind, it reminded her of the way her mother had always done the same thing.

'When will he be arriving?' She tried to take an interest in Emily's much-loved nephew.

The other woman skimmed through the contents of the letter again, the writing large and angular, the signature a single G. 'He says some time Saturday morning.'

Leonie nodded. 'Then I'll make sure I'm gone by about nine.'

'Gone?' Emily repeated dazedly. 'Gone where?'

'To London for the weekend. You won't want me here when you have your nephew staying.' Leonie frowned over the sketch she was just doing, the little boy's dog looking more like a Shetland pony than an Old English Sheepdog. She worked better without interruptions, but dear Emily did like to sit and have a

chat. If only her sketches would come as easily as
Emily's talent for storytelling. But it didn't, her own
minor talent needed much work and sheer hard slog
before she had attained her now high standard. But
not today, this dog just wasn't right at all.

'Nonsense,' Emily quickly disabused her of the need
to go away for the weekend. 'You're like part of the
family. Besides, Giles has expressed a wish to meet you.'

Leonie's huge pansy-blue eyes widened. 'To meet
me? Whatever for?'

'I have no idea. He says—ah, here we are—he says
"I look forward with extreme interest to making the
acquaintance of your good friend Leonora". There!'
Emily beamed. 'Now you can't disappoint Giles,' she
said as if that settled the matter.

Leonie could indeed disappoint him, in fact she had
no choice. And she felt sure that nephew Giles's 'extreme interest' was in fact only a polite acknowledgement of that fact that he knew she even existed. Leonie
had seen the chatty letters Emily wrote her nephew,
and she had noticed the way Emily was always quoting
her. If Giles was the bumptious prig she thought he
was then he wasn't in the least interested in the opin-
ions of his aunt's working colleague. But poor Emily
didn't seem to realise that, insisting that Giles liked to
receive her letters. The fact that she only received
answers to one in every three never seemed to bother
her.

'I have to, Emily,' she lessened the disappointment
with a smile. 'Don't you remember, I told you weeks
ago I would be away this weekend?'

Emily looked vague. 'Did you?'

'Yes,' Leonie insisted patiently. 'My brother is
coming home.' She bit her lip. 'I said I'd go and see
him on Saturday.'

'So you did. Oh, bother!' Emily looked annoyed. 'And I did so want you to meet Giles. I'm sure the two of you will get along famously.'

'Another time,' Leonie excused, sure that she and Giles wouldn't get along 'famously' at all. Giles probably put everyone he met through his own private trial, and Leonie had had enough of courtrooms to last her a lifetime. 'I'm sure there will be other opportunities for us to meet,' she added politely.

Emily obviously wasn't pleased, although she remained very excited about her nephew's visit, throwing the whole house into an uproar as she made ready for his arrival.

By Saturday morning Leonie was pleased to get away, and get her battered Mini out of the garage. As she drove down the long driveway she had to veer sharply to the left; the huge monster of a car coming in the opposite direction was not willing to give an inch as it whooshed past her. She turned to glare at the driver of the Rolls-Royce, receiving only a glimpse of the back of a dark head, as the driver had not given her a second glance.

That had to be nephew Giles, she knew Emily wasn't expecting anyone else this morning. At least Emily would be pleased, he had arrived earlier than she had expected. But as far as Leonie was concerned his manners could use a little working on.

She forgot all about nephew Giles, her thoughts going forward to Phil. She hadn't seen him for four years. He had refused all her offers to visit him, so she had no idea of his reaction to her going to see him this weekend.

He didn't seem to understand why she wanted to see him, telling her in the two letters she had received from him in the last four years that it would be better if

they didn't meet again. Phil felt guilty about his treatment of her, she realised that, but he was the only
relative she had left in the world.

Four years ... God, it was a lifetime! Four years
when she had had to live with the knowledge that Phil,
her stepbrother, had used the love she felt for Jeremy
Lindsay for his own ends. She had gone out with
Jeremy in all innocence, a naïve eighteen-year-old to
his sophisticated forty, never guessing that he was
married, that he had a daughter a year younger than
she was.

But Phil had known, and he had tried to capitalise
on it. The first Leonie had known of his interference
in her life had been when Jeremy had suddenly stopped
seeing her, his haughty secretary always putting her
off when she called him, telling her he was busy or
that he wasn't in the office. The next thing to happen
had been her own and Phil's arrest—for blackmail! The
fact that she had denied all knowledge of Phil's intention, and that he had backed her claim, had made no
difference to the police. She had been charged along
with Phil.

And J. G. Noble had crucified her in court. Oh, he
had been so charming to start with, smiling at her,
pretending he believed her—and then he had pounced. All
the charm had gone, the warm grey eyes turned flinty, his
magnetic good looks became harsh as he verbally ripped
her to shreds—and she hadn't been able to do a thing
about it.

She hated John Noble with a fierceness that hadn't
abated with time, hated the way he had sneered at her
morals, the way he had derided her. She had watched
the blaze of fury in his eyes as she was set free, the
court believing her plea of innocence.

But she would never forget her shame, never forget

the humiliation she had suffered in that courtroom as the intimate details of her friendship with Jeremy were revealed to everyone in the room. J. G. Noble had taken great pleasure in telling of every single kiss, every caress she had ever shared with Jeremy, had watched with contempt as she squirmed in her seat, her face bright red.

Jeremy had been in court too, sitting beside a pretty redhaired woman, his wife for the last twenty years. Leonie had believed him when he told her he loved her, had willingly succumbed to his practised seduction. Just how practised she had soon found out. Apparently the Lindsays were one of those couples who had an 'open' marriage, each partner indulging in the odd affair while still remaining married to each other. Leonie had just been another affair to Jeremy, whereas she had believed him to be the love of her life.

Her love had died as surely as all trust in the male gender had died, and over the years she had built a wall around her emotions that was as hard as steel. Only Tom had ever been able to penetrate that shell, dear sweet Tom who had asked for nothing except that she be his wife.

Almost in London now, she looked up the address Phil had given her, although it still took some finding. Phil had a room in one of the old houses that were still very much a part of London, the rent seeming exorbitant to Leonie. But as Phil had pointed out in his letter, beggars couldn't be choosers.

The house was definitely not what she would have called luxurious, although the decor seemed quite good for a house of this age. By the time she reached the third floor she had passed one room with a child screaming at the top of its lungs, and the room just below Phil's had pop music blaring out so loudly it was impossible to identify song or singer. The place was a madhouse!

There was no answer to her first knock, although she could hear some signs of movement as she knocked again. The door opened slowly and a bleary-eyed Phil stood in the doorway.

He was a vastly changed Phil, his boyish features seeming to have hardened, his face gaunt. There was an air of aggression about him that made it difficult for Leonie to relate him to the boy she had grown up hero-worshipping.

She had adored him all her life, had trailed after him as a child with big worshipping eyes. When he had gone away to university she had been heartbroken, her joy immense when he had suddenly arrived home again a year later. Her mother and father had been furious, and at the time Leonie hadn't realised the seriousness of his being thrown out. She realised now that he had always had a wild restless streak in him, a craving for danger and excitement. Her parents hadn't understood his behaviour at all, and when he moved to London they had been secretly relieved.

But Leonie and Phil had remained close through the years, had become even more important to each other when their parents were killed in a plane crash. She had even travelled up some weekends from the little Berkshire village she had lived in all her life to stay in London with Phil. It had been during one of these visits that she had met Jeremy at a party. He had been so much older than her, so sophisticated and self-assured that she hadn't stood a chance when he had singled her out for his attention.

'Leonie . . .' Phil greeted her now, leaning heavily on the door, wearing only a towelling robe.

She gave a shaky smile. 'I—er—I said I'd call on

you today. Did you get my letter?'

'Yes, I got it,' he acknowledged gruffly, his blond good looks harsh. He was in need of a shave and a shower, although he seemed unconcerned by his appearance.

Leonie bit her lip, her blue eyes deeply shadowed, her bottom lip trembling. She felt strangely vulnerable standing here—and very unwelcome. Phil's mood was resentful, as it had been the first time they had met. She had been four and he twelve, their parents having just married each other and so made them brother and sister. It had taken years for Phil to accept her as such, and now it looked as if he no longer wanted to continue such an unreal relationship as stepbrother and stepsister.

'Aren't you pleased to see me, Phil?' she asked tremulously.

'I told you not to come, Leonie,' he scowled.

'But——'

'Phil, are you coming back to bed?' called a husky female voice.

Colour flooded Leonie's cheeks. She hadn't thought of him not being alone or still in bed—after all, it was nearly lunchtime. 'I'm sorry,' she said jerkily. 'I didn't realise . . .' She turned away, tears in her eyes.

A hand came out to grasp her wrist as Phil pulled her round to face him. 'What did you expect, Leonie?' he taunted. 'I've been away from women for the last four years.'

'Yes.' Her eyes were haunted.

He moved impatiently, his features twisted into bitterness. 'Stop trying to make me feel guilty. You always could, you know, just with one glance from those baby blue eyes. Even when we were younger I succumbed to those blue eyes and your hair like the gold of an angel.' He touched it gently. 'You used to wear it long, Leonie, why did you have it cut?'

She swallowed hard, aware that they were tentatively reaching out towards each other. 'Tom thought it was prettier this way,' she faltered.

'Tom? Oh yes, your husband.' Phil ran a tired hand across his eyes. 'Why did you come here, Leonie? I asked you not to. We don't have anything to say to each other.'

She put her hand on his arm, her fingers long and tapered, the nails kept short for her work. 'You're my brother, Phil,' her eyes implored him. 'Of course I'd want to see you.'

'I'm not your brother, I'm not even related to you, your mother just happened to marry my father.' He shook off her hand.

'Phil!' The female voice was petulant now.

He gave a deep sigh. 'Now isn't convenient, Leonie,' he said tersely, glancing pointedly behind him.

'No,' she agreed huskily.

'Look, I'll meet you in—say, an hour. There's a café just down the road from here, Pete's it's called. Go and have a cup of coffee and I'll see you there later.'

Leonie turned away, feeling slightly sick. Phil had changed, toughened, his mood very bitter. And that he wasn't pleased to see her was obvious.

'Leonie!' Phil's voice was sharp as he halted her.

She turned slowly. 'Yes?'

'Will you be there?' Some of his boyish charm broke through, some of the Phil she had grown up with.

'Do you want me to be?'

'Yes,' the admission was forced out of him.

'All right,' she gave a shaky smile. 'An hour.'

She was sitting at a window table when Phil arrived at the café fifty minutes later, having already drunk two cups of coffee, receiving curious looks from the waitress as she continued to sit here. Phil looked a little better now, freshly shaven, his overlong hair combed into some sort of order.

He sat down opposite her, searching her pale features. 'I'm sorry, Leonie,' he said huskily. 'I ought to be shot. After all this time you still cared enough to come here, and I act like the swine I am. I really am sorry, Leonie, for everything.'

'I know that.'

'I don't see how,' he grimaced. 'I've done nothing to give you that impression.'

'You're my brother—You are, Phil,' she insisted as he went to protest. 'Mum and Dad would have wanted us to stick together.'

'Not after what I did to you. And that bastard Noble!' he swore savagely. 'God, he was a vindictive swine! I'll never forget the way he talked to you, the way he made you appear no better than a——'

'Yes, Phil,' she interrupted with a shiver; Phil had voiced the painful memories she had thought of only hours ago. 'I've never forgotten him either.'

'Handsome devil, wasn't he?'

Leonie looked startled. She had never thought of the lawyer as being handsome, had only ever had nightmares about the condemnation in his accusing grey eyes, the rest of the man had faded into a haze. But she thought of him now, remembered the black hair, the way even at thirty-five he already had grey wings of colour at his temples. His eyes had been piercing, his nose slightly aquiline, with a thin mouth, the lower lip slightly sensual although kept firmly in check. He was a tall man, who had always worn a pin-striped black suit to court, his linen immaculate, his hands long and tapered, the nails kept short and clean.

He had been a man untainted by crime himself, and had no patience or pity with anyone who was. He believed her to be guilty and so she was, it was as simple as that.

'Leonie?' Phil prompted at her continued silence.

She gave a quick, nervous smile. 'Sorry—bad memories.'

'I'm not surprised,' he grimaced. 'He made mince-meat of you. Still, I'm glad you got off in the end.'

'We aren't here to talk about me, Phil,' she said briskly. 'I want to know how you are.'

He shrugged. 'Unemployed.'

She sighed, 'I didn't mean that.'

'I know, love. I'm fine. A little older, a lot wiser.'

'Really?' Her look was piercing.

'Really. Oh, I know it didn't look that way this morning, but Wanda is a special friend.'

'You don't have to explain that to me. It has nothing to do with me.'

'Yes, it does.' He fidgeted with the salt-pot in the middle of the table. 'I was damn rude to you earlier.'

'It doesn't matter.' Nothing mattered now except that she and Phil were actually talking to each other again. After this morning she hadn't thought it was possible.

'It matters.' He put the salt-pot down, looking at her across the table. 'You're my little sister, Leonie. I wish you didn't have to see me like this. And you should hate me—I used you.'

'I don't hate you.' She put her hand over his. 'I never could. Jeremy wasn't what I thought he was anyway. Although that doesn't excuse what you did,' she added hastily.

'If it's any consolation, I paid for it, Leonie. It's no picnic being in jail.'

'No, I'm sure.' He didn't exactly look as if he had been having a good time.

'How's your life been?' He studied her. 'You're looking well.'

Looks can be deceptive. Oh, she was attractive enough, her hair was short and wavy, very blonde, her eyes deeply blue and fringed by long dark lashes, her nose small and pert, her mouth wide and generous, her neck long and slender, her figure petite in the brown silky dress, her legs long and shapely, shown to advantage in high-heeled sandals. And yet she wasn't happy, the wide and generous mouth hardly ever smiled, and there was an unhappy droop to her slender shoulders.

'What was your husband like?' Phil asked at her continued silence.

'Kind,' she replied without hesitation.

'And?'

'And we were very happy together.' She looked down at her empty coffee cup.

'You didn't answer my first question,' Phil prompted softly. 'What was he like?'

'He was—older than me——'

'How much older?' her stepbrother cut in, his eyes narrowed.

'Quite a bit,' she evaded. 'He was a widower, very lonely, and——'

'You kept each other company,' Phil derided.

'He was kind,' Leonie said firmly.

'But he died.'

'Yes. We—we had been married about a year and he—he had a terminal disease. But at least he was happy at the end, I made sure of that.'

She hadn't wanted to become involved with any man, she had shunned them all, but a year after the trial she had met Tom. He had seemed to need her, and in a way she had needed him. He had taught her to live again, had given her a reason for living, and he had loved her very much, despite knowing the truth about her past.

Phil sat back. 'I wonder what Noble would have made of your marrying a man so much older than you, especially as Tom died only a year later,' he shook his head.

It wasn't hard to imagine John Noble's reaction to that. A man like him would never understand the genuine affection that had prompted her to marry Tom. 'I can imagine,' she grimaced. 'But I wasn't left a rich woman, so at least he couldn't throw that in my face.'

'That man could make a nun look corrupt!'

'Only because he has a mind like a sewer,' Leonie snapped.

'You really hate him, don't you?'

'Hate is too mild a word,' she said vehemently. 'What I feel for him can't be put into mere words. And Jeremy was as bad, sitting there with that smug look on his face, letting that man say all those *lies* about me. And they were lies, Phil. I never——'

'I know, love,' he consoled gently. 'I know you too well ever to believe such things of you. If only I'd known of Lindsay's arrangement with his wife! I would never have approached him if I'd known. I'd been gambling heavily, I needed money, and a Harley Street doctor, a married one at that, seemed like a godsend to me.'

'And instead you found he was quite proud of his sexual encounters,' Leonie remembered bitterly. 'It certainly hasn't done his practice much harm. I've heard that he's had to turn new patients away because his book are full—and all of these patients were female,' she added dryly.

'Some women!' Phil scorned. 'The only one who seems to have really suffered out of this is you, and you were completely innocent of the whole thing.'

'I wouldn't call your time in prison getting off lightly.'

'I deserved it. But it's taught me something.'

'What's that?' she asked eagerly.

'Never to get caught again.' He laughed at her expression. 'That was a joke, Leonie.'

She gave a wan smile. 'It's never seemed particularly funny to me.'

'Or me,' he was serious now. 'I really have learnt my lesson. I'd been playing on the edge of crime for some time before Lindsay stopped me. Going to prison was a very unpleasant experience, and I don't intend ever going back again.'

'What will you do about work?' she asked worriedly. 'You said you were unemployed.'

'I'm starting a job on Monday. They got it for me through the prison, so my employers know my background.' He shrugged. 'If they're willing to give me a try then I think I owe it to them to do my best. I'll be a success, Leonie, you'll see.'

'If you need money——'

'No! No, I have enough.' He smiled. 'Just because you're rich now it doesn't mean I'm willing to let you help me out. I have to stand on my own two feet, even if I fall over a couple of times.'

'I'm not rich, Phil,' she smiled at the description. 'But if you need help——'

'I don't,' he told her firmly. 'I'm starting the way I mean to go on, with a clear conscience.' He grinned suddenly. 'But I'll let you buy me lunch if you like.'

'I like,' she smiled back.

They relaxed with each other much more over the meal, laughing together as they used to, and Phil made Leonie feel young again, taking her back to the happy childhood they had shared together.

'When did you start drawing?' Phil asked as they finished their meal. 'I remember you were always good at art, but you never mentioned taking it up as a profession.'

'That was Tom's idea. He was an art teacher at one of the colleges, and he encouraged me to develop what talent I have.'

'It seems to have paid off.'

'Yes.' Much more successfully than she had ever imagined.

'What's Emily Dryer like? God, do you know I can remember reading her books way back in my childhood,' he said ruefully. 'I used to like the way the kids in her stories could always get filthy dirty and get away with it. Mum and Dad used to give me a good hiding if I came home like that.'

'Only because you used to do it all the time,' Leonie smiled. 'And Emily is the kindest woman I ever knew. Next to Mum she's the woman I love the best.'

'Then she must be nice.'

'She is,' she confirmed huskily. 'A little on the forgetful side now, but absolutely full of energy. She leaves me standing when we go for a walk together, and at the end of the day when I'm ready to collapse she's still going strong. The woman she used to work with died, and for a while Emily stopped working. But she has too much talent to stop for ever, and so six months ago she took up her pen again. She had two other girls helping her before me, and neither of them worked out, but when we met everything seemed to click into place.' Leonie shrugged. 'I'm happy there.'

'And you've put the past behind you?'

She repressed a shiver, the past had never seemed so painful as it had been today. First there had been the fact that Emily's nephew was a lawyer, and then seeing Phil again after all this time, both had reminded her very strongly of the past, of the nightmares that were never far away. The past could never be forgotten, it could only be accepted, and she was nowhere near accepting it yet.

'I'm happy,' she evaded a direct answer. 'And especially so now I have you back,' she smiled at him. 'Can we spend the evening together, or are you going out?'

'With Wanda, you mean?' he grimaced. 'She thought you were another girl-friend this morning. It took some time to convince her you were my sister.' His face darkened. 'I could have killed Noble for implying any other sort of relationship between us!'

Leonie had forgotten that, forgotten John Noble's implication that her relationship with Phil was more than just that of stepbrother and stepsister, the way he had hinted at them being lovers and preying on the affections of a besotted man. God, she thought, that man's mind was worse than a sewer, it was totally warped.

'So we can spend the evening together.' She pushed all thoughts of John Noble to the back of her mind, wishing she could forget about him altogether.

'And tomorrow too, if you like,' Phil took his cue from her.

In the end they spent all of the weekend together, and Leonie was glad to discover that Phil's veneer of toughness was only skin-deep, that underneath he was still her much-loved brother. By the time she drove back to Kent she was a lot more relaxed, and Phil seemed more inclined to seeing her again.

She was surprised to see the plum-coloured Rolls-Royce still in the driveway when she arrived back at Rose Cottage late on Sunday evening. She smiled to herself as she remembered the way she had looked for Emily's cottage when she had come down for the first meeting, only to discover that the 'cottage' was a huge house, albeit surrounded by a veritable orchard of roses. Emily was an eccentric, and if she wanted to call her home Rose Cottage then that was exactly what she could call it.

Leonie let herself into the house with her own key, hearing the murmur of voices in the lounge. She would have to go in and say hello to Emily's nephew, although after that long drive she wasn't really in the mood to be sociable.

Emily came out of the lounge, closing the door behind her. She smiled as she saw Leonie. 'There you are, my dear. I was getting quite worried about you. Did you have a nice time with your brother?'

'Lovely, thank you, Emily.' She slipped off her jacket, the navy blue trousers and blouse she had worn for the drive still looking bandbox fresh. 'Have you had a nice weekend?'

'Oh yes,' Emily glowed. 'I'm just going to make some coffee, would you like some?'

'Let me do it,' Leonie instantly offered.

'Certainly not,' Emily replied indignantly. 'I'm perfectly capable of making a pot of coffee. You're as bad as Giles! I'm not incapable, you know. He says I should slow down, that I work too hard.'

'Well, you do,' she agreed gruffly, knowing Emily wasn't going to like her saying it.

'I *have* to work, it's what I like doing best.' She sighed. 'Now I'm not going to let you upset me. Go

along into the lounge and introduce yourself to Giles.'
She marched off into the kitchen.

With a shrug Leonie turned to open the lounge door.
Emily's last words had bordered on an order, and it
sounded as if her nephew might have upset her once
today already. Emily was a dear, but she didn't like
criticism of any kind, especially about the hours she
worked. Obviously nephew Giles had touched upon
this sensitive subject.

A man rose from the chair beside the fire as Leonie
entered the room, a man who left her gasping, a man
who was shockingly familiar, a man with the cruellest
eyes she had ever seen, and that man was John Noble!

CHAPTER TWO

'You!' His eyes went black with recognition, his expression one of unsuppressed fury.

Leonie was deathly white, almost a sickly grey. It was like all her nightmares coming true in one terror-stricken minute. The chances of her ever meeting John Noble again had been highly unlikely, and yet here he was in Emily Dryer's lounge, could in reality only be Emily's dearly loved nephew Giles.

He looked much older, the wings of grey hair at his temples more pronounced, although at thirty-nine this was only to be expected; his eyes were more flinty than she remembered, his mouth more cruel, his face all strong angles, his body lean in the dark grey trousers and black fitted shirt. He was tall and powerful, and he towered over Leonie like an avenging angel.

He took a step towards her, the savagery in his face increasing as she flinched away from him. He caught hold of her arm, his fingers digging painfully into her flesh. 'What are you doing here?' he demanded angrily. 'What are you doing in my aunt's house?'

Her hope that perhaps there had been some ghastly mistake, that perhaps this wasn't nephew Giles went crumbled into the dust. Nephew Giles and John Noble were the same man! If she could have said anything at all in that moment it would probably have come out as an hysterical laugh, but her voice seemed locked in her throat, only her eyes able to mirror her fear and shock, her utter terror.

'Answer me, damn you!' He shook her hard, uncaring of the bruises he was inflicting through the silkiness of her blouse.

Whether she would finally have been able to speak she never afterwards knew, for at that moment Emily bustled into the room, the tray of coffee in her hands. For all his fury John Noble was still able to move forward and take the tray from his ageing aunt, placing it on the low table that stood in front of the sofa.

'I wasn't long, was I?' Emily chattered as she poured out the three cups of coffee. 'Have the two of you introduced yourselves?' She looked up enquiringly.

Leonie swallowed hard, sure that she must look terrible. 'I——'

'No,' John Noble said tautly. 'No, we haven't.' His expression was grim as it raked mercilessly over Leonie's slender figure.

She twisted her hands nervously together under that insolent appraisal, wishing she could tell what he was thinking, but his thoughts were as enigmatic today as they had been in court four years ago. If anything he looked even more haughty, more arrogant.

'This is my nephew Giles, Leonora,' said Emily with a smile, unaware of the waves of antagonism passing between the other two. 'He's John really,' she confided. 'But as his father was also called John we've always called him Giles.'

Except in court! In court he had been John G. Noble. Well, at least now she knew what the G. stood for! This man, this hateful, sarcastically cruel man, was Emily's beloved nephew. Either Emily was unaware of the harshness in him or else she knew of it and excused it. Knowing Emily it would be the latter, she always had sympathy and understanding for the unpleasant quirks in people's natures.

'And this is Leonora,' she announced proudly.

'Leonora . . .?' Giles Noble raised an enquiring eyebrow.

'Carter,' Leonie supplied in a stilted voice.

His piercing gaze went to the simple gold band that encircled her wedding finger. 'Ah yes,' he drawled. 'You're a widow.'

'Leonora lost her husband two years ago,' his aunt supplied. 'Such a shame for one so young.'

'Yes.' Giles took the proffered cup of coffee. 'When you spoke of your widowed friend Leonora, Aunt, I naturally assumed her to be a—lady of your own age.'

'Did you, dear?' Emily said vaguely. 'But I'm sure I mentioned how young and pretty she is.'

'No, you never did.' Giles Noble's mouth twisted, his gaze rapier-sharp as it raked over every inch of Leonie's body.

He was doing it again, but now he was stripping her not only of her pride but of her clothes too. She had never seen that insultingly familiar look in any man's eyes before, never felt such degradation at a man's glance. Her humiliation was complete as with a contemptuous twist of his lips he turned away.

'Oh well, it doesn't matter,' his aunt smiled brightly. 'I'm sure the two of you will be good friends.'

Leonie almost choked over her coffee at the unlikelihood of that happening. Her hand shook as she returned the cup to its saucer, her fear a tangible thing. This man was her tormenter, the evoker of all her night-time fears, and yet she could feel his magnetism as strongly as she had in the courtroom, knew that once again he was swallowing her up, absorbing her personality, reducing her to the naïve child she had still been four years ago when she first met him.

Giles Noble looked at her again. 'My aunt tells me

you've been to see your brother this weekend. I believe he has been—away?' his voice taunted her.

'I—er—Yes.' She stared down at her hands, her breath catching in her throat as she waited for him to speak again, for that cold clipped voice that could be silkily soft when he wanted it to be to rip into her once again.

'Where?' he asked finally.

She drew a ragged breath, raising her head slowly. 'He's been—working abroad,' her eyes met his challengingly. 'On an oil-rig,' she added defiantly.

'Really?' Giles Noble drawled slowly. 'How interesting—for him.'

Leonie swallowed hard. 'Yes.'

'Why don't you both sit down?' Emily asked from the sofa. 'I don't like you both towering over me like this.'

'Sorry, Aunt. Mrs Carter . . .?' He waited for Leonie to be seated before sitting himself, his long legs stretched out in front of him, his position relaxed.

Leonie sat in a daze, wondering why he didn't just expose her to his aunt. He knew damned well Phil hadn't been working abroad, he could do his arithmetic as well as he did everything else, and he knew very well Phil had just been released from prison. And yet he said nothing. What sort of cat-and-mouse game was he playing with her now?

'I'm sure you can call her Leonie, Giles,' Emily was still unaware of the tension between them. 'Can't he, dear?'

'Leonie?' he repeated softly. 'But I thought your name was Leonora?'

She bit her lip. 'It is. Emily just—prefers to call me that.'

'It's too pretty to shorten,' Emily put in.

'Most people call me Leonie,' she said firmly.

'Do they indeed?' Giles slowly drawled.

'Yes!' she snapped, her tension almost at breaking point.

'Then so shall I. You see, dear Aunt, I happen to think Leonie is a much prettier name.'

Thank goodness for that. She could still remember the contemptuous way he had called her Leonora in court. At least she was to be spared that.

'Does your brother enjoy his work on the oil-rig?' Giles Noble asked suddenly.

Leonie visibly jumped, the question unexpected—as he had known it would be. He was still the lawyer, throwing her off guard, tricking her. 'He's left now. He has a job in London.' Why didn't he just say that he knew it was all a pack of lies, that her stepbrother was a jail-bird?

He nodded, his expression mocking. 'You'll be able to see more of him, one presumes.'

'Yes.'

'That will be nice, for both of you. I'm sure it can't have been all that comfortable where he's been.'

'Don't be silly, dear,' his aunt chided. 'They have all the conveniences on those places nowadays.'

'So they do,' he gave a slight smile, even white teeth visible between those firm lips. 'Except women. I suppose your brother was living it up this weekend?'

Leonie gave him a cold look, the memory of Wanda in Phil's room still an embarrassing one. 'We spent a quiet weekend together,' she informed him resentfully.

Those firm lips tightened, the eyes glacial. 'I'm sure you did.'

'I don't like to hurry you, Giles,' his aunt cut in, 'but it's after eleven, and you have a long drive in front of you. I do wish you would leave it until morning, I don't like to think of you driving all that way in the dark.'

Giles stretched his long legs. 'I do it all the time when you don't know about it, Aunt Emily.'

'Well, I know, but the point of that is that I *don't* know about it. I shall only worry,' she added persuasively.

'Actually, Aunt, I've been thinking of taking you up on your offer to stay an extra night. I don't have to be in court until tomorrow afternoon, I could drive up after breakfast.'

'Oh, that's a splendid idea!' his aunt clapped her hands together with pleasure. I'll just go up and check that Dorothy hasn't stripped your bed. She has a habit of getting things done before you want her to.' She bustled out of the room, a worried frown on her brow.

Leonie gulped, glancing over at Giles Noble, hurriedly looking away again as she saw he was looking right back at her, his expression unreadable.

Suddenly he stood up, his movements restless. 'Of course you know why I'm staying on,' he said coldly.

'Yes,' Leonie didn't attempt to prevaricate.

'So your brother is out of prison now,' he remarked quietly.

'I'm surprised you remember us,' she said tautly. 'After all, you've prosecuted in much more important cases than ours.'

'But I've never lost one that was quite so cut and dried,' he told her contemptuously.

'You didn't lose,' she gasped. 'Phil went to prison because of you.'

'And you walked away free.' His eyes were narrowed.

'But not because of you,' she scorned.

'No, you would have got life if I'd had my way!'

'Life?' she repeated dazedly. 'Even if I had been guilty, which I wasn't, I certainly didn't deserve life!'

'I happen to think you did.'

'That was obvious,' Leonie snapped.

'You were guilty, Leonie.'

Her eyes flashed. 'The court didn't seem to agree with you.'

He shrugged. 'Unfortunately they can't always be right. Most of the time, yes, but not always.'

'This time they were!' she told him vehemently.

His look was dismissive of such a claim. 'The wedding ring on your finger, is it real?'

'Of course it's real! You——'

'You mean there *was* a Mr Carter?' He sounded sceptical.

'Yes, there was a Mr Carter!'

'And he walked out on you.'

'No, he *died*. You already know I'm a widow.'

'You've lied before, you could be lying now. I had no idea my aunt's friend Leonora was really Leonora Gordon, the girl who——'

'Mr Noble,' Leonie cut in stiffly, 'my past is my affair. The fact that you happen to know about it shouldn't make any difference.'

'But it does,' he said silkily soft. 'Don't you think my aunt is entitled to know that her trusted friend was once prosecuted by me on behalf of her lover?'

'He was not my lover!' she denied heatedly, her initial fear now fading to anger. She didn't have to take this abuse from him, she was no longer on trial.

'Wasn't he?' Giles Noble's mouth twisted scornfully. 'Jeremy tells a different story.'

'I'm sure he does,' she said disgustedly. 'He has a reputation to maintain.'

'You aren't trying to tell me that he made all that up? Because if you are I should save your breath; he went into the affair in great detail. I probably know as much about you as he does.'

Leonie's face blazed with colour and she felt sick. She had allowed Jeremy to touch her more intimately than any other man had done, might even eventually have slept with him, but she hadn't. She hadn't! That he had invented the details of their affair she knew, and it was obvious that Giles Noble believed every word.

'Why should his story be any more believable than mine?' she challenged. 'It takes two, you know.'

'So I heard.' Once again his mouth twisted with contempt.

'Mr Noble——'

Emily came back into the room, beaming at them both. 'For once Dorothy hasn't been quite so efficient. Your bed is still made up, Giles.'

'Then I suggest we all retire for the night,' he said smoothly, showing none of his animosity towards Leonie in front of his aunt.

Leonie was only too glad to go to bed, although she couldn't sleep once she was prepared for bed, pacing the room as she wondered what Giles Noble's next move would be. She was surprised he hadn't given her away to his aunt at once, although his remark about his aunt being entitled to know seemed to point to him not being silent for much longer.

What would happen when he told Emily, dear kind Emily who tried never to believe a bad word about anyone? Well, she couldn't be sacked, not directly, she was contracted by the publishing company and not by Emily herself, and yet things could be made so unpleasant for her here that she would have to leave. And if she left she would be in breach of contract. Because Emily couldn't work without her illustrator in residence it had been written into Leonie's contract that she had to live at Rose Cottage. At the time of signing the contract she hadn't minded moving in here, but now it wouldn't be possible for her to stay.

She still hadn't got over the shock of seeing John Giles Noble again. She must have had a premonition of this meeting, why else had he been so much in her thoughts the last few days? He had it within his power to hurt her unbearably, to strip her of all the quiet happiness she had managed to attain for herself the last few years. All her security had been taken from her in a single moment. At the first glimpse of those steely grey eyes after four years she had known that Giles Noble wouldn't let her escape without making her suffer all that humiliation once again.

She spun around as her bedroom door slowly opened, her eyes opening wide as Giles Noble quietly entered. He closed the door behind him, leaning back against it, his arms folded across his chest. Leonie pulled her silky bathrobe more securely about her, making sure the belt was firmly tied. Not that she feared any moves from him in that direction, he had made his contempt of her very clear. No, it had been an involuntary action on her part, and one that seemed to give him amusement.

'What do you want?' she demanded.

'What sort of question is that to ask the man who's just entered your bedroom?' he drawled, moving to slowly look around the bedroom she had made her own.

'*This* man, a very relevant one,' she retorted in an angry whisper. 'And could you lower your voice, your aunt may hear us?'

Giles shrugged, picking up her black lacy bra from the chair and putting it down again with a quirk of his eyebrows. 'I don't need to talk at all,' he said softly. 'Neither of us does—unless you're one of those women who like to talk.'

Leonie gasped. 'What do you mean?'

'Jeremy told me all about you, Leonie.' He was advancing towards her like a predator after its prey, and for once those grey eyes were not icy but held a warm glowing invitation.

'If he told you *all* about me then you should know whether or not I like to talk,' she scorned to hide her fear. This was the last thing she had been expecting from this man, and she didn't know how to cope with it—unless she was sick all over him. She couldn't allow him to touch her, she cringed just at the thought of it.

'He didn't mention it.' Giles's eyes were on her parted lips. 'But he mentioned a lot of other things.'

'I'm sure he did. Did he also mention that he's a liar?' she said shrilly.

'Oh, come on, Leonie, isn't it time you stopped this game now?'

'Game?' she swallowed hard. 'What game?'

'Four years ago we were attracted to each other.' He was standing so close to her now his thighs were touching hers. 'Don't make me wait any longer to touch you.'

'T-touch me?'

'Yes.' His hand ran from her breast to her thigh. 'You're more slender than you were then,' he looked down at her breasts, slowly raising his eyes to her face, 'but just as beautiful. Leonie . . .'

She was galvanised into action at the sight of his dark head lowering to hers, flinching away from him, her disgust evident in her face. 'Keep away from me!'

she spat the words at him. 'Don't *ever* touch me again! Attracted to you?' she swallowed down the nausea. 'I can't bear you near me. You—you make my skin crawl!'

He was breathing heavily, his expression savage. 'You might lie to yourself, Leonie, but don't bother to lie to me. You wanted me before and you want me now.'

'Never!' Her eyes were wide with fear as he advanced on her yet again. 'I don't want you. I don't!' she cried brokenly. 'If you touch me again I swear I'll be sick!'

His eyes blazed at her challenge, his mouth twisted with cruel satisfaction. 'Maybe you like to fight— something else Jeremy didn't tell me,' he drawled insultingly.

'Do you know him so well he would discuss such things with you?' she said disgustedly.

'About you he told me everything.'

'More than everything, by the sound of it! If you don't get out of my room, Mr Noble, I'm going to scream so loud I'll wake the whole household. Do you want that?'

He gave her a considering look. 'Now why would you do a thing like that? We haven't even discussed the details yet. I'll make the same arrangements for you that Jeremy did. Satisfied?'

Leonie frowned. 'What arrangements?'

Giles shrugged. 'The apartment, the car, the monthly allowance. Of course, it will be a bigger allowance than he gave you—after all, nearly five years have elapsed since your affair with him.'

She gasped. 'You really believe all that rubbish about the car and the allowance?'

He nodded. 'And don't forget the apartment.'

'I never stayed at that apartment. Jeremy may have

paid the rent on it, may even have taken other girls there, but I never even saw the place, let alone actually lived there.'

'The maid said differently.'

'A maid employed by Jeremy! Don't you see, it was all made up, to blacken my character even more.'

'Let's forget about Jeremy, for God's sake!'

'Forget him!' Leonie echoed shrilly. 'Do you think I haven't tried?' And yet his handsome face was much harder to bring to mind then Giles Noble's, it always had been; this man's image was indelibly printed on her memory. 'I despise him, and I despise you even more for listening to his lies. Now would you please get out of here?'

'No,' he replied calmly.

'I shall scream,' she threatened again.

'Go ahead.'

She got no farther than opening her mouth, when his firm lips instantly clamped down on hers. Leonie had never known such faintness, everything started to fade into darkness, her body going slack, and still that mouth continued its punishing onslaught, moving over the softness of her lips with a savagery that bruised.

When she felt she could take no more he at last raised his head, his eyes searching her waxen features, her dilated eyes and shaking body. That she was suffering from a minor form of shock was obvious at a glance, and Giles's features hardened angrily.

'You really mean it about feeling sick, don't you?' he rasped.

Her breathing was shallow, her eyes dazed. 'Yes,' she choked.

'Sit down.' He led her over to a chair, forcing her to sit down. 'Bend down. That's it,' he put her head between her knees. 'All right?' he asked a few seconds later when she had struggled back up to a sitting position.

She had broken out in a cold sweat now, the shaking was getting worse. 'Could you please leave me? I'm sure I'll feel better when you've gone.'

'I'm sure you will,' he agreed grimly. 'But I'm not going anywhere just yet. Come on,' he led her over to the bed. 'I'll help you in,' he rasped as she just stood there in front of him.

Leonie stood motionless as he helped her off with her robe and slipped off her mules, tucking the covers in around her as if she were a little girl.

His thoughts seemed to be running along the same lines. 'You may only be twenty-two, Leonie, but you've done a lot of living in your young life.'

She was in a daze, making no demur as he moved to turn out the light, half expecting the bed to give as he got in beside her. When she heard the door open and close as he left she heaved a sigh of relief, then turned over to sob brokenly into her pillow.

She stayed in her bedroom the next morning, asking Dorothy for the luxury of breakfast in bed. Not that she was particularly hungry, but not eating breakfast at all would cause even more speculation.

The Rolls was still in the driveway when she let herself out of the house at nine-thirty, her intention to go for a walk until Giles Noble had left to go back to London. She couldn't face him again, not after last night's insults. To think that he had actually offered to make her his *mistress*! She still shook at the thought of it.

She walked down the gravel driveway, wearing practical flat shoes, her denims old and faded, her cotton sun-top showing the creamy expanse of her shoulders, finishing abruptly at her waist. She intended cutting across the fields to the river, and would have done so if the plum-coloured Rolls hadn't come to a silent halt beside her.

Giles Noble leant over and pushed open the passenger door. 'Get in,' he ordered grimly.

'I'd rather——'

'Get *in*, Leonie,' he repeated tautly. 'We have to talk, surely you can see that?'

'If it's about last night——'

He gave an impatient sigh and got out of the car to come round and forcibly push her inside. He was soon behind the wheel again, driving off at great speed.

'Could you please slow down?' she finally had to ask, her fingers digging into the edge of the seat as his huge car manoeuvred the small country roads.

His foot at once eased off the accelerator, his shoes of the finest leather, the formal suit he wore in that dark pin-stripe that Leonie remembered so well.

'Don't you ever wear anything else?' she asked without thinking, at once biting her lip. 'I'm sorry,' her voice was stilted, 'I didn't mean to be rude.'

'I take it you mean the suit. I have half a dozen made a year for wearing in court.'

'But surely it doesn't really show under that black flowing thing?'

He gave a wry smile. 'That "black flowing thing" happens to be a dignified part of my profession.'

'Yes.' She repressed a shiver. The black gown he wore in court had often turned him into a bird of prey in her dreams, the gown appearing as wings, wings he wrapped about her before he devoured her. 'Whose life are you hoping to ruin today?' she asked bitterly.

His mouth tightened. 'The man in question is as guilty as hell,' he told her grimly.

'It must be nice to always believe that,' her mouth twisted. 'I wonder how many of them were really innocent.'

'As you were?' he scorned.

'As I was. There's no point in this conversation, Mr Noble. I can't prove my innocence, if I could I would have done so four years ago. Your friend Jeremy is much more believable. It's easier to believe a Harley Street doctor than the young girl who imagined herself in love with him.'

'You didn't love him at all,' Giles said tautly. 'You and your brother used his infatuation with you to try and obtain money from him. How did you feel about seeing Philip Trent this weekend? Did you find you still love him?'

'I've always loved Phil, but not in the way you mean,' she told him resentfully. 'Take me back, Mr Noble. I shall pack my belongings and leave immediately.' Damn the contract, she wouldn't live through this agony again, not again. 'You can explain the reasons for my departure to your aunt.'

'I don't intend telling my aunt anything,' he surprised her by saying.

Leonie gave him a sharp, suspicious glance. 'Why?'

'I never discuss my cases with her. I never discuss them with anyone.'

'But surely this is different? Surely—You don't want to tell her because you still plan to have an affair with me!' she accused heatedly. 'You're hoping to use my past to force me into an affair with you. My God, you're worse than any criminal you'll ever meet in the courtroom!'

His mouth twisted. 'You know damn well that isn't how it's supposed to happen, Leonie.'

'Yes!' she insisted. 'But I won't be forced. No man

will ever use me again, not in any way.'

'Not even Trent?' he taunted harshly. 'Didn't you and he discuss using the same method on me that you used on Jeremy?'

'You?' Leonie's eyes were wide, deep blue eyes the colour of pansies.

'Yes, me,' he confirmed tautly. 'Last night I was just trying to make things easy for you, see how far you were prepared to go at our first meeting. You're an even better actress now than you were four years ago, your outrage seems quite genuine.'

'Maybe that's because it is genuine! You mean you came to my room last night hoping to *trap* me, trying to make me attempt to blackmail *you*?' She was incredulous at the deviousness of this man's mind.

Giles gave her a sideways glance. 'Don't tell me it never crossed your mind.'

'But it didn't!'

'If you had agreed to my suggestion last night I would have been disappointed,' he drawled insultingly. 'I have you marked down as much cleverer than that. I was supposed to be really desperate for you before you agreed to come to me.'

'Come to you . . .?'

He shrugged. 'I'm a prominent barrister, third generation. I would want to protect my reputation and family name at all costs. And it would be a fitting revenge, wouldn't it, Leonie?'

She swallowed hard. 'Revenge . . .?'

'Don't tell me you never thought of revenge.' His mouth twisted.

'Yes, I thought of it!' Her eyes sparkled with hatred. She had thought of revenge many times, until Tom had reasoned that John Noble was just doing his job, that if it hadn't been him it would have been someone else. But he hadn't had to *enjoy* it, hadn't had to be quite so cruelly sadistic!

Giles gave a mocking smile. 'I knew you would. Those huge blue eyes of yours can be so candid on occasion. I saw the hate in them every time I looked at you, saw the anger burning there. You may have changed outwardly, Leonie, assumed a sophisticated veneer, but those eyes are unmistakable. I would have recognised them anywhere.'

'There's no reason why you shouldn't,' she said tightly, trying to take in all that he was saying.

'But you didn't think I would.'

'I didn't?' She wasn't even listening to him any more, her head was aching, her temples throbbing. She would leave here today, would get as far away from him as possible, and would try to build a life for herself—once again.

'You said so yourself last night,' he reminded her. 'Different name, different look—oh no, my recognising you wasn't part of the plan at all. I could see the shock in your face when I showed straight away that I knew you were Leonora Gordon.'

'I was shocked at seeing you, not at being recognised!'

'Oh yes?' he scorned.

'Yes,' she insisted heatedly. 'I had no idea you were Emily's nephew.'

'You're saying she never spoke to you about me?' he derided. 'Even though I know she takes great pride in telling every new acquaintance of how proud she is of me.'

'She wouldn't if she knew what a bastard you are!'

He shrugged. 'She knows, she just chooses to ignore it. You may have noticed, she sees no wrong in anyone.'

'I've noticed,' Leonie muttered. 'But I had no way of knowing that Emily's nephew Giles, and John Noble, were one and the same man. They certainly didn't sound like the same man.' Emily's glowing accounts of her nephew had no bearing on the man Leonie had met in that court four years ago.

'It won't work, Leonie,' Giles drawled mockingly. 'I would never get caught in a trap like that.'

'Too intelligent, I suppose,' she said sarcastically.

'You could say that. Of course, I could have let this charming little charade take its course, and then told you the truth, but that would just be a waste of your time and mine. I'll take you back to the cottage now, I'll even drive you back to London if you still want to go.'

'I don't.' She suddenly came to a decision. She liked it at Rose Cottage, enjoyed her work, and she loved Emily's company, so she wasn't going to be driven away. Tom had taught her to stand firm when she believed in something, and she believed in her right to live her life without interference from Giles Noble.

He raised dark eyebrows. 'Do I take that to mean you've changed your mind about leaving?'

'You can take it how you like, Mr Noble,' she said with saccharine sweetness. 'But I am contracted to work with Emily, and that's exactly what I intend doing.' She looked at him challengingly.

'And if I tell her about you?'

Leonie faced him unflinchingly, suddenly very calm and in control. This man couldn't hurt her any more, and she intended showing him that. 'I'm sure that in her usual fashion she'll skip over the more unpleasant parts and see me only as a girl caught in the force of circumstances. Yes, you go ahead and tell her, Mr

Noble. I really couldn't give a damn any more what
you do.'

'Couldn't you?'

'No! If I have to leave this job I'll just get another
one. You can't touch me any more.'

'We'll see, shall we?' he smiled, a smile without
humour, like a cobra about to strike its victim. 'Yes,
we'll see,' he repeated softly.

CHAPTER THREE

'ARE you telling me you're still there?' Phil was incredulous when she visited him in London a couple of weeks later.

Leonie gave a light laugh. 'Yes, I'm still there.'

'And you've seen nothing of Noble since you parted on that Monday morning?'

'Nothing,' she shook her head.

Leonie had been surprised by that herself, expecting Giles Noble to keep badgering her until she left. Every time the telephone rang she jumped, every time someone knocked on the front door she tensed, but so far there had been no sign of Giles Noble. And he hadn't told Emily a thing about them having met before. This uncertainty was worse than anything, but then he probably knew that. At the moment they were having a war of wills, it was all a question of who broke first. Well, it wasn't going to be her!

Phil raised his eyebrows. 'That's rather strange, isn't it?'

'I think he's hoping I'll just leave.'

'And you aren't going to?'

'No.'

'Why not?'

'Oh, I thought about it, very seriously, in fact. But I'm through running, Phil. If he wants me out then he'll have to throw me out, literally.'

'And you think he won't?'

She gave a half smile. 'I'm sure of it. He would have done it by now if he was going to.'

Phil shook his head. 'I've a good mind to try something on him just to see what would happen.'

'Phil!' Leonie gasped.

He relaxed back on the sofa that he converted into his bed at night. The bed-sitter was infinitely tidier than it had been the last time she had called on him here. And Wanda was noticeably absent too! 'I wouldn't really,' he grinned. 'Although the way it looks you can't really blame him for expecting it.'

'I know that,' she sighed. 'And I don't blame him for that. I just hate the way he tried to trap me into it. The merest suggestion of blackmailing him and he would have had you in prison before you could deny all knowledge of it.'

Phil became serious. 'I'm never going back to prison. Never!'

Leonie bit her lip. 'How's the job going?' she changed the subject to something less sensitive.

He shrugged. 'It's okay. But I'm not going to get very far as a delivery boy.'

'I thought you always wanted to open up your own restaurant,' she frowned.

'I did.'

'If it's a question of money . . .'

'Of course it's a question of money,' he said irritably. 'I'm not exactly a safe bet for a bank loan.'

'Tom didn't leave me destitute, Phil. I could——'

'No!' He stood up to pace the room. 'I won't accept anything from you.'

She looked bewildered. 'But I——'

'Don't you understand, I've taken enough from you already! If I hadn't interfered you would have had your fling with Lindsay, eventually found out what he was really like, and the affair would then have blown itself out. Instead of which the whole thing was made embarrassingly public, and Noble crucified you.'

She touched his arm as he walked past her. 'I'm glad I found out about Jeremy.'

'But I could have just told you about him, you didn't have to find out that way!'

'No more recriminations, Phil, please. Now, about this restaurant——'

'I can't take money from you, Leonie,' he told her firmly.

'But——'

'I said no!'

'All right,' she sighed in the face of his obstinacy. 'I have to go now, Phil, Emily hasn't been too well lately, so I told her I would be back early.'

'What's wrong with her?' he seemed genuinely concerned.

'She's had rheumatism for years. It gives her a lot of pain, but this week has been worse than most. I've had the doctor out, but there's really not a lot he can do except give her something to help her sleep at night.'

'Does Noble know?'

Leonie shook her head. 'She wouldn't have him bothered.' Her mouth twisted. 'She says he's too busy to be worried with something like this.'

Phil shrugged. 'No doubt he is.'

'No doubt,' she agreed bitterly. 'Anyway, I must go.'

'But you'll come again?'

She smiled. 'Of course I will. By the way, how's Wanda?'

'Very well,' he grinned back. 'I'll have to introduce the two of you some time.'

'I'd like that.'

'Really?'

'Really,' she nodded. 'Maybe the next time I come down.'

'Okay, I'll arrange it.'

Leonie drove back through the early evening sun-
light, feeling more relaxed, the beauty of the evening
soothing her. Until this move to Rose Cottage she had
lived in town, in Tom's house, and now she had found
that she liked living in the country most of all, enjoyed
the slowness of life, the clean fresh air.

Dorothy, Emily's housekeeper, came rushing
into the hallway as soon as Leonie entered the
house. 'Oh, Mrs Carter, thank goodness you're
back!'

'What is it?' She was at once concerned. 'Is Emily
all right?'

'She's resting. She had a fall, Mrs Carter, just after
you left this morning. I told her to stay in bed today,
and she said she would, and then the next thing I knew
she'd fallen part way down the stairs.'

'Oh, my God!' Leonie was very pale, instantly blam-
ing herself for going out and leaving Emily on her own.
'Is she upstairs?'

Dorothy nodded. 'In her bed. The doctor said she
has a very badly bruised hip, and that he'll be here
again tomorrow to see how she is.'

Leonie was already part way up the stairs. 'He
should have taken her to hospital. At Emily's age you
can't take risks.'

Dorothy wheezed up the stairs behind her, almost
as old as Emily herself. 'Oh, she's had X-rays and
things. She was at the hospital for hours, but once she
knew there were no bones broken she insisted on
coming straight home.'

'Have you let Mr Noble know?' Leonie lowered her
voice as they reached Emily's bedroom door.

'She wouldn't have him told,' Dorothy whispered
back.

Leonie's eyes widened. 'You mean he doesn't know?'

'No.'

She sighed. 'I'll call him when I've spoken to Emily. You have Mr Noble's telephone number?'

Dorothy nodded. 'On the pad downstairs. But Miss Emily won't like it.'

Leonie smiled. 'I won't tell her.' She turned and let herself quietly into the bedroom, not wanting to disturb the elderly woman if she was sleeping.

The pink and white room was almost in complete darkness, with only a single sidelight to alleviate the gloom. Emily lay back against the elevated pillows, her eyes closed, her even breathing evidence of her sleeping state. For the first time in their acquaintance Leonie saw the other woman looking all of her sixty-two years, her face bare of the powder and lipstick she usually wore, her grey hair slightly ruffled.

Leonie sat with her for several minutes before going back downstairs. She had to let Giles Noble know, no matter what Emily said. Her hands were clammy as she dialled his number, her heartbeat sounding very loud in the silence of the hallway.

'Mr Noble's residence,' answered a stiff formal voice.

Leonie's breath released in a hiss as she realised she wasn't talking to the man himself. At least she had a few moments' respite, enough to try and calm herself before she spoke to Giles Noble. 'Is Mr Noble at home?' she asked breathlessly.

'I'm afraid not,' replied the uncommunicative voice.

Damn. 'Do you have any idea when he will be?'

'Tomorrow evening, madam. Mr Noble is away for the weekend.'

Oh yes—with whom? 'Could you give me a number where I could reach him?'

'I'm afraid not, madam.' The voice was even more stilted, as if the man was surprised at her effrontery in thinking he would reveal his employer's plans to her, a mere voice on the telephone.

Leonie sighed. This obviously wasn't going to be easy. 'But you do know where to reach him?'

'Of course,' the man sounded indignant now.

'I have to know where he is,' she told him firmly. 'His aunt has had a fall, and——'

'Mrs Dryer has?' At least that voice had some emotion to it now.

'Yes.' At least she was getting somewhere. Giles Noble's manservant was more like a watchdog, protecting his employer's privacy at all costs. 'Could you give me his telephone number?' she repeated.

Within seconds she had a number she could call him on, although on trying it she received no answer. She felt totally dissatisfied when she joined Dorothy in the kitchen a few minutes later.

'Try again later,' the housekeeper advised when told of Giles's unavailability. 'Would you care for some dinner now?'

'Why not?' Leonie shrugged.

She tried the telephone number several more times, again receiving no reply. When Emily woke up she went up to keep her company.

'I'm just fine,' Emily assured her. 'A little tired, but then that's only to be expected when I've been pumped full of drugs.'

'Dorothy is getting you something light to eat,' Leonie smiled at her. 'And you must try and eat it.'

'I'll try,' Emily grimaced. 'Although I'm not really hungry.'

'Dorothy will be upset.'

'I know, that's why I'm going to try. I sometimes wonder who runs this household, me or her.'

'Her, I think,' Leonie laughed lightly, relieved to see Emily hadn't lost her sense of humour. Seeing the other woman ill like this had brought home just how fond of her she was, even fonder than she had realised. Not that she thought Emily would be down for long, she was too active for that.

'Now you haven't contacted Giles, have you?' Emily said sternly.

'No,' Leonie replied truthfully. After all, she hadn't actually spoken to him yet.

'Good,' Emily said with satisfaction. 'Because it was only a little fall, certainly nothing to worry him with.'

Emily might not think so, but Leonie had no doubts who Giles would blame for the omission if he wasn't told. She watched over Emily as she ate some of the chicken soup, hiding a smile as Dorothy scolded her for not eating it all. Emily and Dorothy went back a long way, a relationship more like sisters than employer and employee.

Leonie went downstairs once Emily had drifted off to sleep again, taking her sketchbook with her into the lounge so that she could do some work. She was getting behind on her illustrations, had fallen way behind Emily, and mainly because she couldn't concentrate. This battle of wills with Giles Noble was bothering her more than she cared to admit, and no matter how she tried to banish him from her thoughts he was always at the back of her mind, like a dark shadow over her life.

It was after eleven when she heard the voices in the hallway and the slamming of the front door. She stood up slowly, watching as the lounge door was flung open and Giles Noble walked in, resplendent in evening clothes, a raven-haired beauty following him into the room, her dress also pointing to their having been out for the evening.

'How is she?' he demanded without preamble.

'Sleeping.' She couldn't take her eyes off how magnificent he looked in the dark suit and snowy white shirt, almost human in fact. 'How did you know to come?' she asked dazedly.

'You telephoned Davenport, didn't you?' he said tersely, dismissively.

'The manservant? Yes,' she still looked bewildered. 'But I tried the number he gave me several times, the last time only a few minutes ago, and there's been no answer all evening.'

'Sonja—Miss Johnson and I have been out to dinner. Luckily Davenport remembered where we were dining and contacted me there.'

'He might have let me know!'

'I don't suppose it occurred to him.'

'Then perhaps it should have occurred to you,' she snapped. 'I've been worried sick!'

'Did you think something might have happened to me?' he taunted.

Colour flamed in her cheeks. 'I couldn't care less if it had.'

'That's what I thought,' Giles drawled.

'Is this a private conversation,' the woman called Sonja interrupted frostily, 'or can anyone join in?'

Leonie flushed almost guiltily, having momentarily forgotten the presence of a third person. Sonja was a woman in her early, possibly mid-thirties, tall and slender, her make-up perfect. She was beautiful, exquisitely so, although the hardness of her green eyes marred that beauty somewhat.

'Sorry, Sonja,' Giles smiled at her, a warm intimate smile. 'This is my aunt's—associate, Leonie Carter. Leonie, Sonja Johnson.'

'Miss Johnson,' Leonie nodded acknowledgement, not liking the look of the other woman at all. 'I think you aunt may be asleep, Giles,' she deliberately used his first name, watching the way his eyes narrowed suspiciously. 'It was a nasty fall, but I think she's feeling better now.'

'Were you here when it happened? I thought you were going to London this weekend.'

Her eyes widened and then she frowned. 'How did you know that?'

'My aunt told me when I telephoned earlier in the week. I take it you went to see Philip Trent?'

'My stepbrother, yes.'

'Ah yes, your stepbrother,' there was no mistaking his sarcasm. 'Didn't you go in the end?'

'Yes, I went. But I knew Emily wasn't too well, so I——'

'You mean she was ill before the fall?' he interrupted coldly.

'Yes. But——'

'Why didn't you let me know?' again he cut in, angry now. 'You must have realised I would want to know.'

'Emily didn't want you told.'

'That's no damned——'

'Giles,' Sonja Johnson spoke again, 'don't you think you should go and see your aunt and stop chastising Mrs Carter—It is Mrs, isn't it?'

'Yes,' Leonie confirmed tightly, feeling the other woman's dislike.

'I'll go up now,' Giles told them. 'Miss Johnson and I will be staying the night.' He spoke to Leonie, his eyes cold.

'Of course.' She hadn't expected anything else this time of night. 'I'll help Dorothy prepare the rooms—unless of course you only require the one?' she arched an eyebrow enquiringly.

Giles drew an angry breath. 'Two rooms, Leonie,' he said tautly.

'Very well. If you'll excuse me . . .' She left the room, sure that their sleeping arrangements for the night had been planned much differently. Giles had obviously been spending the weekend with Sonja Johnson, and not innocently either.

The first she knew of Giles having followed her was when he roughly swung her round to face him. 'What was that dig about in there?' he demanded angrily, his eyes blazing.

She gave him a look of innocence. 'I just thought it would help prevent your weekend being a complete washout.'

'And just what do you think my aunt would make of that arrangement?' he snapped.

'Oh, she assures me that you have your—friends,' Leonie taunted, enjoying the fury in his face. 'Although I doubt she would expect you to entertain one of them here.'

'You——' he broke off with effort, drawing a deep controlling breath, pushing her away from him. 'You little bitch,' he said with quiet disgust.

She stood her ground. As she had told Phil, she was through with running. 'I'm sorry,' she said with feigned politeness. 'Did I misunderstand the situation?'

'You know damn well you didn't!'

She smiled. 'Yes. Excuse me, I must catch Dorothy before she goes to bed.'

'See if you can arrange some coffee and sandwiches,'

Giles requested tersely. 'Miss Johnson and I didn't have time to finish our meal.'

'Of course,' Leonie inclined her head haughtily. 'The doctor will be out to see your aunt again tomorrow.'

'Right,' he nodded, his thoughts preoccupied.

Leonie found Dorothy just preparing for bed, although she came willingly to help her prepare the two rooms. Leonie let her go to bed after this, preparing the coffee and sandwiches herself. It had been a difficult day for Dorothy, and she looked almost as tired as Emily had earlier.

Sonja Johnson was alone in the lounge when Leonie carried the tray in. Giles was obviously still up with his aunt, which meant Emily must be awake. She poured out two cups of coffee, picking one up before turning to leave the room.

'Please help yourself to cream and sugar, Miss Johnson,' she invited in a stilted voice. 'I'm just taking this up to Emily.' There was no reason for her to be polite to Giles Noble's girl-friend, especially when the other woman looked at her so disdainfully.

'I thought you were helping Giles's aunt with one of her books,' Sonja Johnson said with slow derision. 'I didn't realise you helped around the house too.'

Leonie had to literally bite her tongue to stop the sharp retort that sprang to her lips. She gave a saccharine-sweet smile. 'You might be surprised by what my—duties in this house involve.' She was deliberately provocative.

Anger flashed in those hard green eyes. 'Why, you——'

'I must take this up,' Leonie said firmly. 'I wouldn't want Emily's coffee to get cold.'

She closed the door with a calmness she was far from

feeling. Sonja Johnson looked like proving to be as obnoxious as Giles Noble. At least they were well suited!

Emily gave her a reproving smile when she entered with the coffee. 'You shouldn't have bothered Giles,' she gently reprimanded.

'Yes, she should, Aunt. I would have been very angry if she hadn't.'

Leonie knew that, it had been her main reason for wanting to contact him. She certainly hadn't wanted him down here herself!

Giles sat on the side of his aunt's bed, holding her hands in his much larger ones. His affection for his aunt was unmistakable, but right now Emily looked as if she could do with another sleep. And no wonder— Giles was overwhelming enough to have in anyone's bedroom, as she had found to her cost!

'Drink your coffee while it's still hot, Emily,' she encouraged. 'Giles and I will leave you to rest now.'

Emily looked disappointed. 'But he's only just arrived, Leonora.'

'It's very late,' she said firmly. 'And Giles has some coffee of his own waiting for him downstairs—among other things,' she added for him alone.

Emily's interest quickened. 'Do you have someone with you?' she asked him excitedly.

The look he shot Leonie left her in no doubt of his anger. 'I happened to be dining with someone when I received the message about your fall,' he revealed tightly. 'It would have been rather rude to just desert her.'

'Her?' his aunt's face lit up. 'Have you brought one of your girl-friends to meet me?'

His mouth quirked with humour. 'Sonja isn't a girl, she's a woman. And she's nothing like the girl of sweet innocence you keep telling me to marry. I don't know any women who are sweetly innocent, in my job you don't have much opportunity to meet women like that.'

Leonie flushed at his intended insult towards her, feeling reduced to the level of a woman who walked the streets. 'Then perhaps you should change your profession,' she suggested waspishly.

He gave her a cold glance. 'It's my profession that has taught me never to trust first impressions, or second ones, or even third ones, come to that.'

'Never trust your own judgment, hmm?'

'It isn't always prudent to, and the law is able to determine a criminal so much more easily than a single individual can.'

'But I'm sure you make your own personal judgments on people,' she said with dislike.

'I think it must be hard not to, dear,' Emily remarked seriously. 'After all, a barrister is only human too.'

'Is he?' Leonie couldn't resist asking. 'Well, if you say so, Emily. I think Miss Johnson might be getting lonely, Mr Noble,' she added pointedly.

'Oh yes, Giles,' his aunt smiled. 'You mustn't neglect your guest. Will I get to meet her tomorrow?'

He sighed. 'I should think so, if you're feeling up to it.'

'Oh, I will be,' she said happily. 'In fact I feel a bit of a fraud lying here letting people wait on me.'

'You aren't a fraud, Emily,' Leonie assured her gently. 'Now you must get some rest.'

Giles bent to kiss his aunt on the cheeks. 'We'll see you in the morning.' He followed Leonie out of the room. 'What did you mean by that remark?' he rasped, turning her to face him.

'Which one?' She met his gaze unflinchingly.

'The one about my not being human.'

'I don't remember it being a personal remark,' she mocked. 'It was a general observation.'

His eyes narrowed to icy grey slits. 'How many barristers do you know?'

Her mouth twitched humorously. 'Only one.'

'That's what I thought. I'm human, Leonie,' he told her softly. 'On some occasions very human.'

'I'm sure you never forget your dignity, Mr Noble,' she taunted. 'Not at any time.'

'You think not?' his voice was dangerously soft. 'I never refuse a challenge, Leonie. Never.'

She backed away from him, her eyes wide with fear. 'No . . .'

'Oh yes, Leonie.' He had her pinned up against a door, his hand going around her to turn the door-handle and push her inside. He closed the door quietly behind him. 'The last kiss we shared wasn't very satisfying, try to make this one a little more enjoyable, hmm?'

'No!' Panic entered her voice.

The roughness she had expected from him never materialised; his mouth was almost gentle on hers, tasting her lips with slow drugging caresses, his hands cupping each side of her face his only hold on her.

A strange sensation was washing over her, a sensation she had never felt in any man's arms before. She felt like a rose in bud, each petal flowering at the touch of this man's lips. By the time he raised his head to look down at her Leonie was completely dazed, her lips parted invitingly.

'Giles . . .' she groaned achingly.

His eyes were black with desire. 'Dear God, you're a witch! I haven't seen you for two weeks and yet as soon as I saw you again I wanted you. What is it about you, Leonie, why is it that after four years I still can't get you out of my mind?'

Her eyes were wide as she took in the significance of what he was saying. 'But you said it was a trap before, that you——'

'Giles?' a female voice whispered nearby. 'Giles, is that you?'

'My God, it's Sonja,' he groaned. 'I'd forgotten all about her.'

So had Leonie! She had also forgotten who this man was, forgotten the fear he evoked in her. If she felt fear towards him now it was of a different kind. The hatred she had always associated with Giles Noble was now confused with other emotions, emotions she had no comprehension of. She turned away, utterly confused.

'You'd better go to your—lady friend.'

'Leonie——'

'Giles?' Sonja Johnson hissed impatiently.

'I'll have to go,' he sighed. 'Can I come back later?'

'Later?' Leonie gasped dazedly.

'When everyone else is in bed I want to come back and spend the night with you.'

'And Miss Johnson?'

'She won't expect to sleep with me here,' he dismissed easily.

'You're right, Giles,' she spat out. 'You are human on occasion—right now I think you're slightly insane! I'm not spending the night with you now or at any other time.'

His eyes became glacial, his mouth tight. 'You think not?'

'I know it,' she declared adamantly.

'Brave words,' he snorted. 'But I'll break you. You'll become mine, Leonie, and on my terms, if only so that

I can have the satisfaction of getting you out of my system.'

'Mentally you broke me four years ago,' she said dully.

'And now I intend breaking you physically. And that's a promise.'

'Oh, get out of here!'

She knew by the opening and closing of the door that he had indeed gone. She had never felt so lost and bewildered in her life. The man she had hated for the past four years had just kissed her, and unlike the last time, she had *enjoyed* it. How could it be possible to enjoy being kissed by your persecutor? He had said she was a witch, so what did that make him?

Emily stayed in bed again the next day, on doctor's orders, and she did so reluctantly. Leonie wasn't too happy about it either. Oh, she wanted Emily to take care of herself, wanted her to get well, but she didn't welcome the idea of spending the majority of the day with Giles Noble and his lady-friend.

She was just dressing when a knock sounded on her bedroom door. She jumped nervously. Surely Giles wouldn't . . .?

Sonja Johnson opened the door and entered the room. 'Sorry to trouble you.' But she didn't look sorry. 'But I was wondering if I could borrow something of yours to wear today. This dress is hardly suitable for daytime wear.'

Leonie couldn't have agreed more. What there was of the emerald green gown was barely decent. 'Of course, Miss Johnson,' she agreed politely. 'What would you like?'

'Oh, trousers and a top will be fine, anything you can spare.'

Any old rag, Leonie thought angrily. 'I'm not sure any of my trousers would fit you—you're taller than I am,' she added to take the bitchiness out of her words, although the sting was still there. This woman rubbed her up the wrong way at a glance, and she made no secret of her dislike of Leonie.

'A dress, then.' Sonja Johnson swayed gracefully over to the open wardrobe. 'This will be perfect,' and she pulled out Leonie's newest dress, a cream silky sheath, very chic, very sophisticated. She raised those pebble-hard eyes, her mouth curving into a smile. 'Is it all right for me to borrow this?'

'Of course,' Leonie said tightly. She hadn't even worn that dress herself yet! Now she knew she never would, not once this woman had worn it.

'I may as well put it on here.' Sonja began unzipping the green gown.

Leonie busied herself putting on her own casual denims and fitted purple blouse, knowing she was supposed to see the perfection of the well-proportioned body in black bra and briefs, but studiously ignoring the other woman.

'You won't keep him, you know,' Sonja Johnson suddenly spat out, all pretence gone as she glared vehemently at Leonie.

In a way Leonie had been expecting this, had known when the other woman knocked on her door that she must have realised this was the room Giles had left last night. 'I don't want him,' she didn't prevaricate. 'In fact, you're welcome to him.'

For a moment the other woman looked disconcerted, and then she had herself under control again. 'I know what's been going on here,' she snapped. 'But Giles will come back to me when he's finished with you.'

'How nice for you,' Leonie said sweetly. 'But as I

just said, I don't want him.'

'I'll tell him that.'

'You do that, although I think he already knows. Why don't you try asking him?'

'I just might do that!' Sonja flounced out of the room in Leonie's dress, already having made it her own, the cream material clinging to her slightly fuller figure.

But Leonie knew she wouldn't ask him any such thing. Sonja Johnson wasn't at all sure of Giles. In his company she became kittenish and clinging, and Leonie's disgust increased as the day progressed. Giles caught her pained looks a couple of times, and she could see it made him angry.

She had been eyeing him warily all day, although outwardly he acted Emily's polite nephew. But behind that polite mask his grey eyes glittered warningly, his gaze often insolently appraising, his comments barbed.

When he suggested leaving mid-afternoon Leonie heaved a sigh of relief, glad to have his disruptive influence removed once more. It wasn't a relaxing feeling being with someone who had the worst possible opinion of her, a man who had threatened to physically break her.

His goodbyes made to Emily, and Sonja seated in the plum-coloured Rolls-Royce, Giles came back into the house. Leonie had just begun breathing easily for the first time that day, and when she looked up and saw him looming darkly in the doorway her face went white.

She flinched as he came menacingly towards her, a barely leashed violence about him as he pulled her to her feet.

'Did you think you'd got rid of me that easily?' he taunted mockingly.

'I hoped I had,' she trembled against him, swallowing hard.

'I'll be back next weekend—without Sonja,' he added dryly.

'That sounds like a threat,' she quavered, looking up at him like a trapped animal, feeling once again that sensual excitement he had woken within her last night.

'It is,' he said huskily.

Leonie licked her suddenly dry lips. 'I could always leave, disappear.' Even though it was the opposite of what she had said she would do, she knew she would rather leave than have to fight this man every time she saw him.

'This time I'd come after you,' Giles rasped. 'And I'd find you.'

He would, she knew he would. She was trapped! 'I won't leave,' she said dully.

'I know you won't.' His head lowered and his mouth claimed hers, his hands on her spine arching her body to his. The kiss went on and on, Leonie's head spinning, her hands up in the dark thickness of his hair. 'I swear I'll come looking for you if you aren't here next Saturday when I arrive,' he warned her as he put her away from him, then turned and left without a backward glance.

CHAPTER FOUR

'TELEPHONE, Mrs Carter.'

Leonie looked up from the sketch she had been working on most of the afternoon, thanking Dorothy as she went to answer the telephone. She hoped Phil was going to invite her down to London for the weekend; she had to get away, if only for a couple of days. Going to stay with Phil couldn't be classed as running away, not even by Giles Noble.

She snatched up the receiver. 'Oh, Phil, it's so nice to hear from you!' There were tears in her eyes, the last week of worrying about Giles had made her an emotional wreck. 'I hope you've called to ask me down to London with you.' The silence on the line made her frown. 'If it isn't convenient,' she babbled, realising that Phil had a life of his own to lead, 'that's all right, Phil, speak to me!'

'You aren't going to stay with Philip Trent or anyone else this weekend,' a familiar icy voice told her.

Leonie swallowed hard, going deathly pale. 'Giles . . .'

'That's right,' his voice was clipped. 'I called to tell you I'll be there with you in a few hours.'

'But it's only Friday!' Panic coursed through her, a feeling of time running out.

'Maybe I couldn't stay away from you another moment longer,' he drawled.

She could just picture the derision on his face. 'Your aunt will be pleased to see you,' implying she wouldn't! 'She's lying down at the moment, otherwise I'd get her for you.'

64

'You aren't going to escape me, Leonie, so you might as well accept the inevitable. Just think of me as one more man in your bed,' he said insultingly.

'One more——?' she gasped.

'Did your husband know of your other men?' Giles managed to display his disgust even down a telephone line. 'He must have known there was one man, anyway.'

'He must?' she asked dazedly.

'Don't be naïve, Leonie,' he taunted harshly. 'A man always knows when he's the first.'

Of course he did! What an idiot she was! 'Tom knew all about my past,' she told him dully. 'He knew because I told him.'

'Very sensible,' Giles derided. 'So much better than him finding out after the marriage. Was your brother very disappointed about your plans concerning me not working out?' he shot the question at her in the same way he had in court.

'There was no plan.' She frowned.

'Maybe that was the trouble, maybe you would have been better changing your appearance more dramatically, although I still don't think it would have worked. I never forgot you, and Jeremy hasn't either,' he added harshly.

She went white. 'Jeremy? You've spoken to him about me?'

'Plenty of times.'

'What did he say about me? What——'

'We'll discuss it later tonight. I'll look forward to seeing you, Leonie,' and with that cryptic comment he put the telephone down.

She sat down in the chair next to the telephone, biting her lip worriedly. It sounded as if Jeremy had been stirring up even more trouble. She hadn't seen him since the court case had ended, so what could he possibly have told Giles now?

'Anything wrong, dear?' Emily came down the stairs, the limp from her bruised hip hardly noticeable now, although she had been taking things at a slower pace this week.

Leonie took her into the lounge and rang for tea. 'That was Giles,' she managed to say brightly. 'He's going to be here a day early, won't that be nice?'

Emily's face lit up, making Leonie feel guilty about her own reluctance to have Giles here. 'How lovely! But he isn't bringing that dreadful Johnson woman with him, is he?' she asked worriedly.

'He didn't mention it.' But she felt sure the other woman wouldn't be with him, she had definitely cramped his style last week.

'Oh, I do hope he isn't.' Emily looked rueful. 'She may be the first of his women friends he's introduced to me, but I can't say I liked her.'

She spluttered with laughter at Emily's woebegone expression. 'I don't think he expected you to.'

The older woman brightened somewhat. 'You don't?' she said hopefully.

'No,' Leonie smiled.

'Oh, good,' Emily smiled too now. 'I wouldn't want to offend Giles by not liking someone he was particularly fond of. But Miss Johnson was rather—well, overwhelming. She treated me as if I were in my dotage,' she added indignantly.

Treatment of that kind was guaranteed to annoy Emily. Leonie had never known such energy; Emily's age had not seemed to prevent her doing anything she set her mind on.

Leonie was conveniently in her bedroom when the Rolls came to a halt outside the front door. She could hear Emily and Giles in the hallway, and then Giles's firm tread as he came up the stairs, presumably with his overnight bag. She tensed as he seemed to hesitate outside her door, her breath releasing in a hiss as he passed on.

She quickly escaped out of her room before he came back, joining Emily in the lounge for a sherry before dinner.

'Giles is so pleased you're here,' Emily informed her happily.

'Is he?' Leonie tensed.

'Oh yes, very pleased. I'm so glad the two of you like each other. I'd so like——' she broke off, biting her lip. 'There I go interfering again. More sherry, Leonora?'

'No, thank you,' she frowned, her thoughts on the remark Emily hadn't finished. It sounded as if Emily was doing a little matchmaking between Giles and herself. How he would laugh if he knew!

'Ah, there you are, Giles.' Emily was looking past Leonie towards the door. 'And looking so handsome too. I'm sure that isn't on my account,' she added coyly.

Leonie had known he was there before Emily spoke, had felt an electric current shoot through her, an awareness of Giles' eyes upon her. She turned slowly to face him, her eyes widening with shock as she took in the cream suit and brown shirt he wore. He registered her surprise, his eyes frankly mocking her as he came further into the room.

He moved with that slow languid grace Leonie remembered so well, the look in his eyes making her wonder how she had ever thought him cold. His warm gaze swept over her, stripping her naked, bringing an embarrassed flush to her cheeks.

That Emily was aware of this exchange she had no doubt; there was a satisfied smile on the other woman's lips, a glint in her eyes. Yes, Emily was definitely match-making—and Giles was giving her the impression that she was succeeding.

He came to stand beside her, his eyes caressing. 'You look charming, Leonie. Doesn't she, Aunt?'

'She looks beautiful,' his aunt corrected. 'But then she always does.'

'Yes,' he agreed dryly.

Leonie moved jerkily, moved away from the magnetism Giles exerted over her at will. He held a fascination for her that frightened her, and yet in a way she felt bound to him. Perhaps it was because he had stripped her to her soul, had laid bare her slightest emotion, whatever the reason, she felt as if he owned her, that when he decided to claim her she would have no choice but to go to him. In a way he had laid claim to her four years ago, and it seemed that he had now decided to make her his. And she just couldn't fight him!

All through dinner she watched him beneath lowered lashes, and she knew that he watched her too. Emily watched both of them, a look of extreme pleasure on her face.

When she excused herself after dinner Leonie wasn't in the least surprised, she had half expected it. Giles made a token show of stopping her, but it was obviously not meant, and Emily left with a satisfied smile curving her lips.

Giles was instantly beside Leonie on the sofa; soft music came from the stereo, the lights dimmed. 'I thought I was never going to get you alone,' he groaned, pushing her backwards, his body quickly covering hers, his thighs already hardened to passion.

She didn't fight his mouth on hers, in fact she met him half way. This lightning passion between them was too strong to fight, flaring up whenever they met. And right now it was a blaze, their breathing ragged, their hands pushing frustratedly at the clothing that separated them.

'I said you look charming, and you do, but right now I can think of a way you would be even more beautiful,' his mouth moved restlessly over her throat, his hands in her hair. 'You have too many clothes on, Leonie,' he muttered.

'Not too many,' she murmured, slowly unbuttoning his shirt to touch the silky hair beneath, hearing him gasp as she playfully dug her nails into his flesh.

'No, you don't, do you?' He had slipped her dress from her shoulder, baring her breasts, bending to run the tip of his tongue lightly over her rosy nipples.

She gasped, pleasure shooting uncontrollably through her body. She clutched him to her, her hands in the thickness of his hair, increasing the pressure of his mouth on her breast, his teeth gently biting.

When his lips came back to claim hers she met the demand of his passion, easing his jacket from his shoulders, completely unbuttoning his shirt. As their bare torsos met their skin seemed to sear together, her breasts were crushed beneath Giles's weight, and yet it was a pleasurable pain, causing an ache that seemed to be growing and growing.

'Giles,' she groaned breathlessly. 'Oh God, *Giles*!' She was trembling, her whole body shaking.

'Make love to me, Leonie,' he encouraged.

No man had ever invited her to love him in this way, allowing her hands and lips to go where they would; Giles's desire was unhidden from her. She kissed and caressed him, feeling him quiver against her as she bit his taut flesh, loving every hard curve of his chest.

He watched her every move, his breathing shallow. Suddenly he shuddered, a dark flush rising in his cheeks. His hand clasped about her wrist and pulled her away from him. 'No more, Leonie,' he moaned, his eyes momentarily closing. 'I can't control this situation any more.'

'Do you want to?' Her voice was husky, a provocative pout to her lips, her eyes love-drugged.

'No,' he replied softly. 'But I have to. We can't make love here, Leonie. I've waited this long for you, I can wait a few days longer.'

She stiffened, pulling her dress back over her shoulders. 'What do you mean?'

Giles slowly sat up, the tension ebbing from his body. 'We can't conduct an affair here, not under my aunt's roof.'

'Affair . . .?' she echoed dully.

'Yes, affair. I have to have you, despite the fact that I despise you and the methods you use to trap your men. This affair will be on my terms, with no interference from your brother, and when I've finished with you there will be no blackmail attempts made on me,' he told her harshly. 'In the meantime you can stop seeing Trent.'

'Stop seeing him——?' Leonie gasped, staring at him as if he were mad. 'But he's my *brother*!'

Giles stood up. 'He's absolutely no relation to you, and I'm sure you've both remembered that on occasion. Have you slept with him since he came out of prison?' He tucked his buttoned shirt back into the waistband of his trousers.

All her old resentment of him bubbled to the surface, her eyes flashing with burning anger. Seconds after making love to her, after seeming as aroused as she had been, he was insulting her again.

'Leonie?' he prompted an answer from her.

She pushed back her tangled hair. 'I'll see Phil any time I damn well want to,' she snapped.

His hand went around her throat, tightening threateningly. 'Not when you belong to me you won't,' he said tightly.

'Belong——?' She moved out of his grasp, rubbing her bruised flesh. 'I have no intention of belonging to you!' She turned to glare at him. 'And Phil and I have *never* slept together.'

'That isn't what your friend Jeremy said.' Giles straightened his ruffled hair, pulling on his jacket, looking for all the world as if that passionate scene between them had never happened. 'He told me the two of you slept together all the time.'

'Jeremy again!' she said fiercely, her hands clenched into fists. 'Why do you believe everything he says?'

'Because,' he came to stand beside her, 'these lie,' he gently tapped her lips, his hands running insolently down her body, 'but this doesn't,' he laughed as she shuddered against his touch. 'You like a man's hands on your body, in fact you love it.'

She loved his hands on her, no other man's. But she hated *him*! He would pay for his treatment of her. It was time someone paid for the wrong done to her four years ago, and Giles was *it*.

'You think I want you, Giles?' she asked in a subdued voice, her lids lowered to cover her blazing blue eyes.

He gave a husky laugh. 'I know you do.'

She put her hand daringly on his thigh, instantly feeling the surge of desire that shot through his body. 'And do you want me?'

His amusement had faded, his breathing again ragged. He pressed her hand against him. 'You know I do,' his voice was rough with desire.

'How long have you wanted me, Giles?'

'Since you walked into that courtroom four years ago. That's a hell of a long time to wait for any woman,' he added ruefully.

'Did Jeremy give such a good account of my—abilities?' How she kept her voice seductively soft she never knew. She just wanted to hit him. Well, any moment now she *was* going to hit him, and with something more than her hand.

'Not good enough,' he drawled. 'You're better, much better than he said you were. But then,' he shrugged dismissively, 'you're four years older, and you've also been married. What was your husband like?'

Her mouth tightened. She wouldn't discuss Tom with him, not ever! 'Nothing like you,' she made herself smile invitingly. 'Tell me some more about how you're attracted to me.'

He laughed. 'It's enough that you know about it.' He frowned. 'That first night here, why were you ill?'

She thought fast, forcing a bright smile to her lips. 'It was the shock,' she gave a breathless laugh. 'I hadn't realised I was—attracted to you, and—and that surprised me when I'd been hating you all this time.'

'And now?' His gaze was fixed on her parted lips.

Her hand caressed where it lay, watching the tautening of his features with inner satisfaction. 'How do you think I feel?' she murmured throatily.

His smile was supremely confident. 'You have to come to London as soon as possible. I can't keep coming here, I don't have the time.'

'Not even for me?'

'Not even for you, Leonie. Besides, we don't exactly have—privacy here. My aunt seems to think it's the romance of the century, instead of which it's just——'

'Good old-fashioned sex,' she finished. 'What happens in London? The apartment, the car, the allowance?' Her voice had become brittle.

Giles mouth tightened. 'If that's what you want.'

She took a deep breath. 'No, no, that isn't what I want.'

The steely eyes narrowed. 'You want more?'

Now was her chance, now she could allow her emotions full rein. '*Yes*, I want more! I want *marriage*, Giles,' she told him triumphantly. 'Marriage!' she repeated shrilly.

His eyes had widened incredulously. 'You expect me to *marry* you? To make you my *wife*?'

Her expression was calmly innocent, enjoying herself at his expense. 'Yes,' she told him with a calmness she was far from feeling.

He gave her another look of disbelief, starting to pace the room. '*Marriage?*' He kept darting her those looks of incredulity. 'You have to be joking, Leonie.'

'Do you see anyone laughing?' She met his gaze unflinchingly.

'Well, I'm certainly not!' He sounded furious.

'Neither am I.'

'Are you really serious about this?' He stopped pacing to stare at her.

'Very serious,' she nodded.

'You don't expect me to agree, do you?'

She knew he wouldn't, that was why she had suggested it. Giles would never allow himself to marry a woman like he believed her to be, his pride just wouldn't allow it, no matter how much his body clamoured for hers. She knew that, and he knew it too.

'Are you going to?' she challenged.

'You know damn well I'm not,' he said fiercely, his

eyes alive with anger.

'Then this finishes here and now.'

'Is this how you got your last husband?' he demanded angrily. 'Don't you give it away free any more?'

Her face blazed with colour and then went deathly white. 'We'll leave my husband out of this,' she said tautly. 'And I've *never* given it away free!'

'No, you haven't, have you?' His tone was savage. 'Why such a high price this time?'

'A mistress is at such a disadvantage,' she told him with feigned nonchalance. 'She has no rights at all, as I learnt with Jeremy.'

'She does now.' His mouth twisted. 'The law now recognises her rights.'

'Only if you live together openly, and I'm sure we wouldn't be doing that.'

'You've certainly done your homework on the subject,' Giles said disgustedly, his hands thrust into his trousers pockets, as if he might hit her if they weren't.

She hadn't at all, it was just that there had been a case in the newspapers a few months ago about a similar situation, and it was only because the woman had lived openly with her lover for a number of years that she was able to claim a settlement from him. Giles would keep any affair between them very much a secret, she knew that.

'A woman has to take care of her interests,' she told Giles calmly. 'Even in this enlightened age.'

'Well, you aren't taking care of your interests with me,' he rasped.

Leonie eyes him enquiringly. 'Do I take that to mean there will be no marriage?'

'You can take it any damned way you like! But I'll still get you, Leonie. You can't help yourself.'

'Just now I was just giving you what you wanted,' she said in a bored voice.

'I haven't had that—yet.'

'You know my price, Giles. Any time you change your mind . . .' she stood up, 'just give me a call.' She trailed her fingers tauntingly down his hard cheek, feeling at any moment as if the bared white teeth would open up and snap into her tender flesh. But they didn't, and she swayed gracefully over to the door, conscious that he watched her every move. 'Goodnight, Giles,' she mocked. 'Sweet dreams,' and she smilingly closed the door after her, the smile instantly fading.

The arrogant devil! She had never felt so angry, or so violent. She could quite cheerfully have hit him—except that she felt sure he would have hit her back. But she had soon wiped that smile from his face, that air of self-satisfaction. She could almost have laughed at the expression on his face when she had told him she would accept nothing less than marriage. Shock was too mild a word to describe his reaction.

Once in her bedroom she locked the door, just as a precaution. Giles had been angry enough to do anything, but she didn't think that would include breaking down a door in his aunt's house.

Her movements were jerky as she removed her make-up, her anger still a tangible thing. Arrogant, insulting swine! He—Her movements stilled and she collapsed down on her folded arms. She had let *Giles* kiss and touch her, had been like putty in his hands. Harsh sobs racked her slender body, her blonde curls falling forward over her face.

The door-handle rattled softly behind her. 'Leonie?' came the whispered query. 'Leonie, open this door!'

She shrank back against the dressing-table. 'Go to hell!' she told Giles in a fierce whisper.

There was silence for several seconds. 'Leonie, are you crying?' he asked disbelievingly.

'I wouldn't cry over a bastard like you!' She spoilt it all by sniffing, impatiently wiping her cheeks dry of tears. At least she had already removed her mascara and that hadn't run all over her face!

He rattled the door again. 'Let me in. We have to talk.'

'We've talked. I have nothing more to say to you on the matter. Goodnight,' she said for the second time that evening.

'Leonie——'

'Good*night*!'

She heaved a sigh of relief when he at last moved away and she could hear his bedroom door opening and closing. That was it; she would have to get away, at least until Giles had gone back to London.

Emily was very upset about her decision to go to London for the weekend. 'I was hoping you and Giles would take this opportunity to get to know each other better,' she sighed.

If they got to know each other better than they had last night then they would be lovers! Poor Emily, she didn't know how to hide her disappointment at the ruin of her plans. 'Phil has tickets for the theatre tonight,' she invented. 'I couldn't possibly let him down.'

Emily frowned. 'You didn't say anything about this yesterday.'

Leonie smiled. 'That's because I didn't know yesterday. I just called Phil and he's managed to get two cancellation tickets.' The bit about telephoning him wasn't a lie, he just hadn't been at home. Or he had still been asleep, which was more likely, after all it was only nine-thirty, and on a Saturday too.

Emily watched her as she put on her jacket. 'Can't you even wait until Giles gets back? He would be sorry to miss you.'

Leonie's eyes widened. 'He isn't here?'

'He's out walking. Dorothy said he went out very early this morning. He should be back soon.'

All the more reason for her to leave now! And the reason for his insomnia wasn't too hard to guess. He had wanted her very badly last night, and she doubted he was a man who denied himself anything he wanted that much. 'I can't wait, Emily,' she said. 'I want to get to London before lunch.'

'You and Giles didn't fall out last night, did you?' Emily blushed. 'I mean——'

'Of course we didn't, Emily,' she hastened to reassure her. 'But I can't let my brother down.'

'No, I understand that. Oh well,' Emily sighed defeat, 'I'll make your excuses to Giles, shall I?'

'Yes, do that,' Leonie smiled. 'And tell him I was very sorry to have missed him.' She could just imagine Giles's face when his aunt passed on this message. 'Now I must dash, Emily,' she kissed the other woman affectionately on her powdered cheek. 'I'll see you late tomorrow.'

So Giles had been unable to sleep, had he? It served him damn well right! Much as she hated to admit it, she had had some trouble sleeping herself.

She went straight to Phil's bed-sitter, needing his down-to-earth attitude to help her sort out the mess she found herself in. Phil would soon make sense of it all.

'Forget your key——? Leonie!' Phil looked taken aback by her presence outside his door. 'I didn't expect you today. Come in,' he invited, stepping back to allow her entry. 'Now, what's the matter?' he asked gently.

'Matter?' she echoed sharply.

'I know you, Leonie. You're strung up like a coil. So tell me.'

Her bottom lip trembled uncontrollably, her eyes filling with tears. 'Oh, Phil!' She launched herself into his arms.

He let her cry for a while. 'Noble again?' he finally prompted.

She nodded. 'It was awful! He—he——'

'My God!' Phil help her at arms' length. 'He didn't make love to you?'

'Phil?' Her mouth quivered, her cheeks tear-stained. 'What do you mean?'

He sighed. 'He wants you, doesn't he?'

'How did you——?' She turned away, her face fiery red. 'How did you know that?'

'That he fancies you?' Phil shrugged. 'I've always known. The way he used to look at you in court . . . oh, it was obvious.'

'Then why didn't I guess?'

'Because he didn't want you to. He's an expert at hiding his true feelings. Did he make love to you?'

She bit her lip. 'Not quite.'

'Not . . .? Leonie!'

She swallowed hard, moving away from him. 'I'm so confused, Phil. The last time he pretended to want me to see if I would attempt to blackmail him, he even made love to me——'

'You didn't tell me about that,' Phil scowled.

'It was embarrassing. He—he humiliated me!'

'Because you responded to him?' Phil's eyes were narrowed.

'Not that time!' Hot colour flooded her cheeks and she bit her lip painfully. 'I meant——'

'You meant not that time,' he cut in. 'So which time did you respond?'

'Phil——'

He smiled at her embarrassment. 'It isn't a crime to want someone, Leonie.'

'Someone like *him* it is,' she snapped.

'Okay, so you're ashamed of being attracted to him, but ignoring it won't make it any less a fact.'

'But *him*, Phil!' She shook her head with disgust.

'Any man. We can't dictate our chemical reaction to people. So when did you respond?'

'I—Last night,' she admitted dully. 'This time he suggested we start an affair in earnest.'

He raised his eyebrows. 'And——?'

'I turned him down.'

'I see.'

Suddenly she grinned, once again seeing Giles' face when she had made her condition. 'I told him I wouldn't settle for anything less than marriage.'

Phil looked as stunned as Giles had. 'Did you mean it?' he asked in a strangulated voice.

'At the time, yes. He was very insulting. I had to hit back somehow.'

Humour suddenly broke out in Phil's boyish face. 'I bet that knocked him for six!'

'And the rest,' Leonie chuckled. 'I think he's still suffering from the shock.'

'I shouldn't be at all surprised. You——'

'I'm back, Phil,' a familiar female voice called out happily. The girl Leonie realised must be Wanda appeared in the open doorway, a vivacious redhead with laughing green eyes. She gave Leonie a puzzled look. 'I'm sorry, I didn't realise you had company.' She moved slowly to put the shopping bag on the worktop.

Leonie knew it was up to her to break this tableau. She smiled warmly, instantly liking the look of the other girl. 'I'm not exactly company, I'm Phil's sister. And you must be Wanda. I'm pleased to meet you.'

A friendly smile appeared on the other girl's face. 'I'm pleased to meet you too. Phil's told me a lot about you.' She gave a husky laugh. 'All nice things.'

'Then he hasn't been telling the truth.' They all laughed and Leonie could feel the tension easing.

'I'll make us all some lunch,' Wanda suggested. 'Is chicken salad all right with you?' she asked Leonie.

'I couldn't possibly——'

'That's fine, Wanda,' Phil interrupted firmly. 'The chicken is already cooked, Leonie, a whole chicken, so you aren't taking any food away from us.'

'Well, if you're sure . . .'

'We're sure,' Wanda insisted. 'I'll make us a cup of coffee first.'

'Can I be of any help?' Leonie offered.

'I don't have much to do, actually.' Wanda's voice was pleasant, well-educated. 'And there isn't room over here for two.' She was working in the small kitchen area. 'You sit down and chat to Phil.'

'Leonie was just telling me how she propositioned Giles Noble,' Phil drawled. 'She asked him to marry her.'

'Phil!' Leonie protested, looking awkwardly at the other girl.

Wanda looked curiously excited. 'Did you really?'

'No——'

'She did,' Phil chuckled his delight. 'It's all right, Leonie, Wanda knows all about it.'

Leonie was bright red. 'All of it?'

'Most of it,' the other girl answered gently. 'I've known Phil a long time.'

Leonie found that hard to believe. Wanda only looked her own age or maybe a little younger, which meant she could only have been seventeen or eighteen when Phil went away.

'Did you really ask *Giles* to marry you?' Wanda wanted to know.

'Not exactly.' She frowned. 'You sound as if you know him.'

'Slightly.' Wanda concentrated on cutting up the salad stuff.

'Oh.' Leonie was dissatisfied with the other girl's answer, but Wanda didn't look prepared to reveal any more. She turned to look at Phil. 'When I arrived——'

'I thought you were Wanda,' he finished for her. 'That's your cue to ask if we're living together,' he said dryly.

'We are,' Wanda cut in firmly. 'Well . . . we are when he'll let me.'

'You have your key, you come and go as you please,' Phil told her.

'I please to stay,' Wanda confided in Leonie.

'Despite my telling her to go,' Phil said moodily. 'You know you shouldn't be here. If your parents——'

'Damn my parents!'

'Don't they approve?' Leonie could quite understand them feeling slightly nervous of Phil's past, but that was what it was—his past, and it bore no relation to the responsible man he was now.

'They don't know,' Wanda revealed reluctantly. 'They've always done what they wanted, and I intend doing the same. I don't care what they think of my seeing Phil.'

'Of course you do,' Phil disagreed angrily. 'They're your parents——'

'It doesn't bother me! You—I'm sorry, Leonie,' she

sighed. 'Phil and I have had this argument so many times.'

'You know why,' he growled moodily.

'But your sister doesn't,' Wanda snapped, her face alive with anger. 'You might as well know, Leonie——'

'No!' Phil said forcefully. 'Wanda, don't!'

She sighed. 'Leonie has to know some time. I meant it about marrying you, Phil, so it's only fair your sister should know who her sister-in-law is going to be.'

'I don't remember asking you to marry me,' he scowled.

'You didn't. I *told* you we're getting married.'

'Isn't that the man's role any more?'

'Not when the man is as proud as you are. You see, Leonie,' she took a deep breath, 'my name is Lindsay.'

'Lindsay?' Leonie echoed dazedly.

'Yes. My father is Jeremy Lindsay.'

CHAPTER FIVE

WANDA was *Jeremy's* daughter! The daughter Leonie had discovered he had when she was humiliated in that courtroom. No wonder Phil had tried to silence the other girl; he must have known the shock it would be to her.

Wanda came over to her. 'Oh, I'm sorry, Leonie.' She sighed. 'I didn't mean to upset you——'

'Then why the hell did you have to tell her?' Phil rasped. 'She didn't have to know now. She——'

'I did, Phil,' Leonie spoke for the first time, her voice shaky. 'And Wanda's right, it's better to tell me now. Tell me about it,' she invited huskily, controlling her tears with difficulty.

Phil was prowling the room like a caged lion. 'There isn't much to tell. The situation speaks for itself.'

She bit her lip. 'But how did you meet? How did you come to fall in love?'

'Don't you think I'm lovable?' He attempted to lighten the mood.

'You know you are,' she gave the ghost of a smile in answer to his teasing. 'Too lovable on occasions. You used to get away with murder when we were children.'

'Leonie,' Wanda gave her an appealing look, 'do you hate me?'

She looked startled. 'Of course not!'

'But my father——'

'Is not you,' Leonie told her firmly. 'I just found it hard to believe at first. I'm all right now.'

'No thanks to you, numbskull,' Phil snapped at

Wanda. 'You could have been a bit more tactful.'

'I didn't know there *was* a tactful way of telling Leonie that my father was the swine who attempted to seduce her when she was only eighteen,' she said caustically. 'My parents' extra-marital affairs have always sickened me,' she added with disgust. 'They should have just got a divorce and been done with it. Their behaviour can hardly be classed as a marriage. And I grew up in the middle of that!'

Leonie shrugged. 'Maybe it works for them.'

'It doesn't work for the children who have to grow up in that atmosphere. As soon as I saw Phil I knew he was the man for me, and I haven't looked at another man since, not even when he was away. My mother and father can't even go for a week without hunting out some new quarry.'

'You knew Phil *before* all this trouble?' Leonie was incredulous.

'Just,' Wanda confirmed. 'I saw him talking to Daddy one day, and after that I made sure I met him. I pressured him relentlessly to go out with me until at last he gave in. When my father prosecuted Phil I moved out. I meet my parents occasionally for lunch, but other than that I stay out of their lives—and they stay out of mine. They don't know anything about my seeing Phil. And personally I don't think it's any of their business.'

'Oh, come on,' Phil derided. 'You're their only child, of course it's their business.'

'I don't think so,' she flushed. 'Anyway, they wouldn't understand.'

'I wouldn't understand if you were my daughter either,' he exploded.

'Our daughter,' Wanda corrected. 'Any children you have are going to be mine too.'

'You see what it's like,' Phil groaned to Leonie. 'I can't shake her off!'

Leonie smiled at his expression. 'I don't really think you want to.'

'Maybe not,' he acknowledged grudgingly. 'Her letters and visits have been very welcome over the last four years. Your letters have too, Leonie. I just couldn't bear for you to come and see me in that place.'

'I wanted to come and see you,' Wanda spoke to her, 'to explain, but Phil wouldn't let me. I think he was secretly hoping to get rid of me. But I kept coming back. I even took a Cordon Bleu course so that I could help him run this dream restaurant of his.'

'And that's all it is, a dream,' he dismissed roughly. 'I'll never be able to get that sort of money together.'

'Phil, I could——'

'No, Leonie,' he told her firmly. 'I've already told you no. Anyway, you don't have the sort of money we would need to get started.'

'How much?'

'Thousands.'

'How many?' she persisted.

'About a hundred to have the collateral to get the capital we would need. To open a restaurant in London you have to have the money to make it into something really special.'

'You're right, I don't have that sort of money,' she said dully. 'Twenty, maybe, but a hundred ... I don't have that much,' she shook her head regretfully.

'Of course you don't. And even if you did I don't see why you should give it to us,' Phil dismissed with a shrug.

'It wouldn't be a question of giving it to you.' She knew he would never accept that. 'I could have been your partner. But it's a lot of money . . .'

'It certainly is. Is the lunch ready yet, Wanda? I'm starving!' He grinned, the subject of the restaurant forgotten.

'It's ready,' she smiled at him. 'And now we can all eat with a clear conscience.'

Wanda's cookery course obviously hadn't been a waste of time; the chicken was succulent and tender, the salad tossed in a dressing Leonie found delicious.

'Only cheese for dessert, I'm afraid,' Wanda apologised. 'I'm working as a teacher at the moment, and Phil's job doesn't pay too well, so we eat nourishing but cheap foods.'

'Cheese is fine,' Leonie accepted, wishing the other couple weren't quite so proud. But they seemed happy together, which made up for any luxuries they couldn't afford.

'She's trying to keep me healthy,' Phil grinned.

'You certainly look better.' Leonie had noted how his skin was less sallow, a little more flesh on his bones. 'Fitter too,' she teased.

Wanda prepared the coffee, grinding the beans, their aroma filling the room. 'Our one extravagance,' she smiled. 'I love what I call "real" coffee.'

'So do I.' Leonie accepted a cup.

Wanda sat down. 'You haven't finished telling me about your proposal to Giles yet,' she said with repressed eagerness.

'I didn't exactly propose,' Leonie blushed. 'It was a put-off.' She explained the situation to the other girl.

'Goodness,' Wanda's eyes glowed, 'that big virile man after you! I wish I had your luck.'

'I thought you said you loved only me,' Phil mocked.

'I had a crush on Giles when I was about fifteen. I remember he rebuffed me quite gently.'

'So you do know him better than "slightly",' Leonie prompted.

Wanda nodded. 'He and Daddy have been friends for years. In fact it wouldn't surprise me if he and Mummy didn't have something going for them once.'

'Wanda!' Phil warned.

'Well, they might have done.'

'Which means they probably didn't.'

She sighed. 'I was only speculating.'

'Well, don't,' he ordered sharply. 'Can't you see it's upsetting Leonie?'

'It isn't upsetting me,' Leonie instantly denied, aware that that wasn't the truth. It did upset her to think of Giles and the beautiful Glenda Lindsay once having an affair, as it upset her to think of him and Sonja Johnson together. The reason it bothered her was too deep to fathom—and she wasn't sure she wanted to know. It was enough to know that all her past resentment had turned to attraction, any other emotions were better left alone.

'You aren't a very good liar, Leonie,' her brother chided.

'That's funny, Giles thinks I'm a very good liar,' she said with forced brightness. 'In fact, he thinks I do little else.'

'That sounds like Giles,' Wanda grimaced. 'I can never understand why he and Daddy are friends, they're complete opposites. Giles is direct, honest, believes the law should be strictly adhered to, whereas Daddy—well, I'm sure I don't have to tell you anything about my father.'

'Phil was in the wrong, you know,' Leonie pointed out gently. 'He had no right to do what he did.'

'Oh, I know that. But my father had no right to treat you the way he did either. There've been a string of girls since then, you know. And still Giles doesn't seem to realise what sort of man my father is.'

'Oh, I think he knows, he just thinks I'm worse than your father. And on the face of it I suppose I am.'

Wanda frowned. 'He still thinks those awful things about you?'

'Yes.'

'Knowing how sensible he is I would have thought he would have realised by now that you're too sweet and nice to have been involved in blackmail.'

'Maybe his vision is blurred by lust,' Phil taunted.

'Phil!' Wanda admonished.

'Well, is it, Leonie?' he asked.

She blushed, biting her bottom lip. After last night she had no doubt of the depth of Giles' desire for her, he had been unable to control it.

'Your face tells the answer,' Phil smiled. 'Do you want to have an affair with him, Leonie?'

'And know all the time that he's expecting me to extort money from him?' she derided. 'No, thanks!'

He raised his eyebrows. 'So you do want to have an affair with him?'

'No!'

'Yes,' he insisted gently. 'Why don't you just give in to what you feel? If you want him——'

'You don't understand!' Her movements were agitated, her hands kneading together. 'He said to me—he said a man always knows when he's the first.' She blushed at the intimacy of this conversation.

'Yes,' Phil frowned his puzzlement.

'Well, he—he would be!' She raised distressed blue eyes, looking very young and vulnerable.

'Are you telling me——'

'Yes!'

'But your husband——'

'Was paralysed. Tom was ill with a terminal disease, and he'd been in a wheelchair for two years before I met him. I—I loved him as I might have loved a friend.'

Phil whistled through his teeth. 'Then you're still——'

'Untouched.' She nodded. 'After what had happened I didn't want any man within touching distance. Tom was always kind, never demanding, and we were happy together. But it just wasn't possible for him to—to—— We did try, in the beginning, but it never worked out between us.'

'My God, Leonie,' Phil shook his head. 'You certainly play with fire! What if Noble had taken you up on your offer of marriage?'

She shrugged. 'Then he would have got rather a shock on our wedding night.'

'More than a shock, I should think,' Wanda put in dryly. 'Then my father—you and he——'

'No!' Leonie denied heatedly.

'Then no wonder he was annoyed enough to take you to court. My father doesn't like to be told no.'

'You sound as if you're glad he was,' Leonie frowned.

'On this occasion, yes. I'm only sorry he hurt you as he did.'

'Don't be. He may have done the initial hurting, but Giles is the one who carried it on. But if he wants me that badly he's going to have to marry me first.'

'You really would go through with it? Phil was incredulous.

She nodded. 'I really would. If only to see his face when he realised the truth.'

And she meant it. If Giles wanted her that badly he would have to pay the asking price. It appeared he didn't want her, having been long gone by the time she got back to Rose Cottage.

She had spent the weekend with Phil and Wanda, had learnt that despite the unorthodox upbringing her parents had given her she was very much in love with Phil and determined to become his wife. They were obviously very much in love with each other, and Leonie was glad for them, knew that Wanda's vivaciousness was exactly what Phil needed.

'Have a nice time, dear?' Emily asked the next morning, having been in bed when Leonie arrived home the previous evening.

'Lovely. Did you?'

'Once Giles got over his disappointment at your not being here,' Emily gave her a coy glance.

Leonie stiffened. 'I'm sure he wasn't disappointed at all,' she said lightly.

'Oh, but he was, Leonora,' Emily insisted. 'Very much so.'

Maybe he had been, but not for the reason Emily thought. Giles hadn't given up on his plans concerning herself, and he was probably angry at her abrupt disappearance.

She shook herself out of her reverie. 'I'm sorry, Emily,' she smiled, realising she had missed what Emily was saying. 'What did you say?'

'Giles has invited me down to London for a little holiday. And he would like you to come with me.' She gave Leonie an expectant look.

'A holiday?' Leonie repeated dazedly, wondering what Giles was up to now. 'But I—I couldn't possibly come!'

'Of course you could, Leonora. A few days in London are just what we both need.'

'But I've only just got back from there,' she protested desperately. Giles was playing games with her again, and on his home ground she would be much more vulnerable.

'Yes, but you didn't do any shopping. I want you to help me choose some new clothes,' Emily said excitedly.

'I'm sure you shouldn't be walking on that hip to that extent yet.'

'My hip is perfectly all right now. Besides, Giles won't be picking us up for several days yet—Wednesday evening, he said.'

'I really couldn't, Emily. You go, I'll stay here and work,' and avoid Giles!

'Don't be silly, dear. We can see Simon while we're there.'

Simon Watts was their publisher, and he had been asking for a meeting with them for the past three weeks, anxious to discuss the progress on the latest book. Emily had produced her trump card, and she knew it. Leonie had no choice but to agree to go to London with her, although she intended showing Giles from the first that this changed nothing.

From the triumph in his steely grey eyes when he called for them on Wednesday evening he knew that he had at last scored a point over her. Her temper sparked into life, her blue eyes flashing.

'You sit in the front with Giles,' Emily insisted as they came out of the house. 'I'll have more room in the back to stretch my legs.'

'But you said your hip was better,' Leonie reminded

her, hating the thought of sitting beside Giles, his mockery evident to her if not to his aunt.

'Oh, it is, dear,' Emily nodded. 'But I shall be much more comfortable in the back.'

'But——'

'What my aunt means, Leonie,' Giles drawled, stowing their cases in the boot of his car, 'is that she'll fall asleep part way through the journey.'

His aunt smiled. 'How well you know me!'

And how well he knew *her*! Giles knew she didn't want to sit in the front beside him, and yet he had manoeuvred things so that she did what he wanted. What else would he manoeuvre her into before the end of this stay at his home?

With the warmth of the evening and the extreme comfort of the car, she wasn't at all surprised when Emily fell asleep; she felt a little that way herself. Except that she couldn't possibly sleep with the disturbing presence of Giles Noble relaxing in the seat beside her, the pin-striped suit once more absent, the fitted navy blue trousers and shirt he wore casual in the extreme.

'What did you hope to achieve by running away?' he asked her suddenly, his voice pitched low. He saw her worried look in Emily's direction. 'Don't worry, she's fast asleep. You haven't answered my question,' he prompted.

'I didn't run away,' she told him tightly. 'I went to see my brother.'

'In other words you ran to your lover,' he drawled insultingly.

'I did——'

'What did he think of your marriage scheme?'

She looked down at her hands. 'He thought I was insane.'

Giles's mouth twisted. 'For once Trent and I seem to be in agreement,' he said dryly.

'How nice!' her voice was sweetly sarcastic.

'And have you now got over your insanity?'

'No,' she said stubbornly. 'I haven't changed my mind, if that's what you mean.'

'It was,' he snapped.

'Well, my offer still stands, at the same price.'

He didn't answer, his hand moving to rest on her denim-clad thigh, kneading the flesh beneath his fingers, his hand moving slowly upwards, past her hip, over the taut flatness of her stomach, hesitating briefly below her breast before he clasped that tightly, painfully, enjoying watching her squirm beneath his touch, smiling as she gasped.

Leonie had tensed at his first touch, feeling her senses swim as his hand continued to caress her body. His hand on her breast, she tried to break away from him, but his hold wouldn't be dislodged. She stopped struggling. 'Let go of me,' she ordered. 'Take your hands off me!' she told him vehemently as he made no move to remove his hand.

'Keep your voice down,' he snapped. 'Do you want to wake my aunt?'

'Yes, if it will make you stop touching me!' She glared angrily at him.

'I'm never going to stop, Leonie,' he said huskily, his hand becoming gentle now, finding the taut nipple through the thin material of her blouse, his thumb caressing the throbbing tip. 'You're mine,' he rasped throatily. 'And one day you'll be prepared to admit it.'

She slapped his hand away. 'You know the price.'

His mouth set in a taut line, his hand returning to the wheel. 'Why are you denying yourself what you so obviously want?'

She blushed at the derision in his voice, had known that he was aware of her response. 'I'm not denying us, you are,' she replied in a studiously calm voice.

'Like hell I am!'

Leonie shrugged. 'We'll have to agree to differ.' Oh, it was so difficult to keep up this act of a mercenary little bitch when what she really wanted to do was give in to the sensual tingle of her body where he had touched her, to know Giles' full possession even though it would mean eventual rejection.

'About what?' came the sleepy response from the back of the car. 'Oh dear,' Emily sighed, sitting up with effort, 'I think I must have fallen asleep for a few minutes.'

'You did, Aunt,' Giles smiled. 'And Leonie and I were discussing—politics.' He shot her a sideways glance.

'Always a dangerous subject,' Emily straightened her hair. 'No two people can ever agree. Besides, they're all a lot of crooks.'

'That's true,' Leonie agreed, returning Giles' taunting look.

She was introduced to Davenport once they reached Giles' home, finding the man just as she had imagined him to be, very tall and thin, with iron-grey hair, his dress and manner impeccable.

It was a beautiful house, set in its own grounds in an exclusive part of London. Inside was the luxury of fitted carpets in every room, antique furniture, even a collection of china ornaments in a special cabinet in the sitting-room. The bedroom she was shown into was in gold and white, the furniture slightly more modern in here, although no less expensive.

It surprised her that Giles had surrounded himself

with so much comfort; he had always appeared to her a man who needed little, a man complete in himself. But there could be no doubt of the luxurious comfort of this house.

She changed for dinner, a deep royal-blue just-below-knee-length dress, styled in the fashion of the moment, the top figure-hugging, the skirt pencil-thin. She looked very tall and slim in it, her eyes an even deeper blue than usual, her hair a riot of golden curls.

When she entered the sitting-room it was to find Giles in there alone, his suit brown as was his tie, the contrasting shirt an attractive tan colour. He looked very dark and attractive, his hair brushed neatly back from his face to rest low down on his collar.

He stood up at her entrance, a glass of whisky in his hand. 'Drink?' he asked politely, his razor-sharp gaze missing nothing of her appearance.

'Just a sherry, thank you.' Her movements were jerky. 'Emily——'

'Is having dinner in her room,' he turned briefly from the drinks cabinet to tell her. 'The journey took more out of her than she'd thought. She's going to have a light dinner on a tray and then have an early night.'

Leonie felt as if the ground were rapidly disappearing beneath her feet, although obviously Giles couldn't have engineered this. But Emily could! It could all be part of the other woman's matchmaking. In the meantime Leonie had to try and get through an evening with Giles, and at a time when she was already aroused by his caresses in the car.

She accepted the sherry with a nervous smile, moving as far away from Giles as possible. That took her over to the cabinet containing the china figurines.

She knew Giles was behind her even before she saw his reflection in the glass of the cabinet, had felt the warmth of his body even though he wasn't touching her, and had smelt the tangy masculine odour of his aftershave. It was one she particularly liked, its heady aroma made her senses reel.

'Are you interested in china?' His breath ruffled the hair at her nape.

'Er—not really. I don't know enough about it, except to think what's pretty and what isn't.' She didn't turn, she daren't, because that would bring her even closer to him. 'Some of these are lovely. I like that one at the back,' she chattered on. 'The one——'

'Leonie,' he groaned, his hand coming about her waist and pulling her back against him, 'you aren't here to talk about my china figurines.' His lips burnt a trail from her nape to her earlobe, biting gently into her soft flesh.

Each time they met their lovemaking continued as if they had never been apart, and each time it was becoming more and more difficult to say no. She wasn't even sure she would have been able to this time, but Davenport's announcement of dinner made it unnecessary. The warmth in Giles' eyes as they were seated opposite each other at the dining-room table seemed to indicate that the encounter in the sitting-room was far from over.

Davenport served them their meal, making it impossible for any but the most general of conversations, so at least Leonie was able to eat her food in peace. But each time she looked up it was to find Giles' burning gaze fixed on her, and he hardly ate anything at all.

'I think Davenport was quite disappointed by our efforts to eat the meal,' she remarked lightly once they had retired to the sitting-room, Giles preferring a brandy to the coffee she had accepted.

His gaze warmed as he looked at her. 'How can I eat when the only appetite I have is for you?'

'Giles!' She jumped nervously.

'Why so surprised, Leonie?' he said tautly. 'You know damned well you're tying me up in knots.'

'I don't mean to.' She looked down at her hands, aware that her own loss of appetite had been due to a deep ache in the bottom of her stomach—and it had nothing to do with feelings of illness!

'I just can't understand you, Leonie.' He stood up to pace the room restlessly. 'Why the hell do you want to be *my* wife? Can you honestly see yourself enjoying the quiet life I lead? The respectable friends, the evenings when I would be working in my study and wouldn't even give you a second thought, but when I wouldn't allow you to go out without me either? Can you honestly see yourself in the role of a barrister's wife?'

If she were the woman he thought her to be, no. But as she was nothing like he imagined her to be she could well see herself enjoying the life he had just described to her, even if it did mean *he* would be her husband.

'Because I can't,' he didn't wait for her to answer. 'I'm not getting caught in the same trap my father did. He married a promiscuous little bitch, and she ran off with another man.'

'She was your mother, Giles!'

'I know who she was,' he sneered. 'I also know *what* she was.'

'But I wouldn't run off with another man,' she gasped.

'You wouldn't be given the chance,' he rasped. 'You

won't be given the chance, because I'm not marrying you. I want to bed you, not wed you.'

'You're crude!'

'I can be a lot cruder. God, Leonie, I can't take much more of this. I want you so much it's driving me mad.' There was a white ring of tension about his mouth, his eyes dark.

'Why don't you visit Miss Johnson in that case, I'm sure she would be glad to ease your frustration,' she said bitchily.

'It isn't Sonja I want. I haven't seen or wanted her since I drove her back to London on that Monday morning.'

'I'm sure that doesn't please her. She assured me I wouldn't get you, after she warned me off you, of course.'

His eyes narrowed. 'When did she do that?'

'It doesn't matter,' she dismissed, feeling guilty about disclosing the other woman's jealousy.

'It matters,' Giles said grimly, grasping her wrist, looming over her as she sat on the sofa. 'When did Sonja talk to you like that?'

Leonie tipped her head back to look at him, unknowingly baring the vunerability of her slender neck. As she saw his mouth so close to her own her breath caught in her throat. 'Giles ...' she groaned achingly.

He at once compelled her back against the cushions, his lean body pressing down into her. His lips devoured her, his mouth deepening the kiss, his hands caressing the curve of her spine. The zip of her dress slowly slid down her back, Giles touching the bareness of her skin, slipping the dress off one shoulder so that his lips might caress her breast, her nipples already swollen with desire.

'You're beautiful,' he breathed against her silken flesh. 'So damned beautiful you make me shake with wanting you.'

And he was shaking, the whole of his body was convulsing with desire. She arched against him as he continued to caress her, his lips now parting hers in an intimate kiss.

'Leonie!' He gasped as she returned his heated caresses. 'Not here,' he groaned. 'Let's go upstairs.'

Her face blazed with colour as she realised that once again she had fallen victim to her own sensuality, that once again she had allowed Giles Noble to touch her more intimately than any other man.

She wrenched out of his arms, standing up to glare down at him, her hands fumbling with the catch of her zip. Passion still burnt in Giles' darkened grey eyes, his hair caressed into disorder by her questing fingers. 'Not anywhere,' she told him harshly. 'You aren't making love to me anywhere, Giles.'

His eyes snapped with anger. 'Aren't I?' he said fiercely, standing up to come menacingly towards her. 'I think I am. I'm thirty-nine, Leonie, not a boy, and I know what I want. I want you, and by God I'm going to take you.'

Leonie backed away, her eyes wide with fear. She had pushed him too far. As he said, he wasn't a boy, he was very much a man, the veneer of tight control completely gone, leaving only the raging desire that he didn't even try to hide.

'Take me?' she attempted to mock him out of his determination. 'You make us sound like a couple of animals,' she scorned.

'We are. The fact that we happen to be the most intelligent of the species doesn't mean our sexual reactions are any different from other animals'.'

'Don't you believe in love?' she tried to divert him even further.

'Yes, I believe in it,' he surprised her by saying. 'But not even the most sentimental of romantics could call what we have love. Sexual attraction explodes between us every time we meet, and I know you're as aware of it as I am, so don't attempt to deny it,' he derided.

'I wasn't going to,' she bit her lip

'Then at least you don't lie to yourself.'

'I don't lie to anyone!'

'You lie to me, almost every time you open your mouth. Thank God it isn't what you *say* that interests me.' He began to advance on her again.

Leonie took a hasty step back, crashing into the cabinet containing the china. She heard several pieces fall over. 'Oh, lord!' she groaned, closing her eyes, dreading what she would see when she dared to turn around. Several pieces had fallen on to their side, and one piece was lying in two pieces. She turned to look pleadingly at Giles. 'I'm so sorry, I didn't mean to. I——'

'It wasn't your fault,' he dismissed stiltedly, moving her out of the way to check the contents, the deep flush of passion fading from his face.

'Let me——'

'Go to bed, Leonie,' he ordered harshly.

'But——'

'*Now* . While I still have the control to let you. Oh, and Leonie,' he stopped her at the door, 'don't make any arrangements to be out tomorrow evening. I'm giving a small dinner party for my aunt and I'm sure she will want you to be there.'

'And I'm sure you would rather I wasn't.'

'On the contrary,' he drawled, 'I can't imagine anything more—pleasant than your company there.'

Leonie made good her escape while she could, sorry that she had been able to do so at the cost of one of those china figurines. They were beautiful, and she had no doubt the one she had broken had been very expensive.

Emily noticed the missing figurine immediately after breakfast, Giles having left long ago for his offices. 'Oh, what a shame!' she looked at the empty space in the cabinet. 'The shepherdess was one of Giles' favourites. Ah, Davenport,' she turned to the manservant as he brought them in a tray of coffee, 'what's happened to the shepherdess?'

'Mr Noble accidentally dropped it, Mrs Dryer,' he replied in his stiff, formal voice. 'It was broken in two, madam.'

Emily frowned. 'That doesn't sound like Giles.'

'No, madam.'

Was it Leonie's imagination or did Davenport give her a reproving look on his way out of the room? Surely he didn't know it was her . . .? 'Giles tells me he's giving a dinner party in your honour this evening,' she rushed into speech.

Emily smiled her pleasure. 'Isn't it lovely of him, so thoughtful.'

'Who will be coming?' Leonie was just glad to be off the subject of the figurine.

'Giles has invited about a dozen people, some of them my friends from when I lived in London, some of them his own friends.'

'Miss Johnson?' Leonie asked dryly.

Emily grimaced. 'Oh no, dear. At least, he didn't mention her. You've worried me now. Now let's see, he said the Andersons, Joe and Maggie Forsythe, Jim Fenton, the Lindsays, Ann and——'

'Lindsay?' she echoed shrilly. 'I'm sorry,' she said more calmly at Emily's concerned look, 'but I used to know someone called Lindsay. I—I just wondered if it was the same person.' Surely Giles couldn't be that cruel!

'Oh, I doubt it, Leonora. Unless of course it was their daughter you knew, she's more your age. Jeremy and Glenda are in their forties.'

He *had* done it to her! Jeremy and his wife would be present at this dinner party tonight. And Giles was going to enjoy watching her squirm!

CHAPTER SIX

'WHY?' Leonie demanded of him tearfully that evening.

Giles loosened his tie before removing it altogether, unbuttoning the top button of his shirt. His jacket had been discarded as soon as he entered the room, the waistcoat to the pin-striped suit fitting smoothly over his taut stomach.

'Why what?' he asked absently, moving to pour himself a huge tumblerful of whisky, which he drank down in one swallow. 'God, what a lousy day!'

Leonie had been waiting in the lounge for him when he got home, ready to do battle. Emily was upstairs in her room resting before preparing for the evening ahead. Giles looked tired, lines of weariness beside his nose and mouth.

'What happened?' she taunted. 'Did an innocent man get off?'

'No, he damn well didn't,' Giles snapped, his eyes narrowed with anger. 'And he should have done.'

'Then appeal,' she shrugged.

'He isn't my client,' he bit out tautly.

Leonie's eyes widened. 'You mean you think the other man should have won?'

His glass landed on the table with a clatter. 'It isn't a question of winning or losing,' he told her grimly. 'It's a matter of justice being carried out. In this case it was wrong.'

'I'm surprised you can admit it,' she scorned.

'I can always admit when I've been wrong.'

'Meaning that in my case you weren't,' she said bitterly.

He shook his head. 'I don't believe so, no.'

'Is that why you're putting me through the humiliating experience of meeting Jeremy again?' she demanded to know.

'So that's what all this is about.' He sighed, and poured himself another glass of whisky. 'Do you want one?' he indicated the array of drinks.

'I *want* to know why you're doing this to me,' she said firmly.

'Curiosity.'

'Curiosity!' Leonie repeated shrilly. 'You're playing around with my life out of *curiosity*? My God, you're a bastard!'

Giles shrugged. 'I want to see if all feeling between the two of you is dead.'

Her eyes flashed deeply blue. 'You didn't need to go through this charade for that, my feelings are very much alive.' She hated Jeremy as much now as she had four years ago.

His expression darkened. 'They are?' he said harshly.

'Yes,' she snapped.

'I see,' he said tightly.

'I hate you for doing this to me, Giles,' her voice shook. 'You must know how embarrassing it will be for me.'

'I'm beginning to,' he rasped, and swallowed some of the whisky, his expression grim.

'And how do you think your friend Jeremy is going to feel when confronted with the woman he once prosecuted?'

'Let's be honest, Leonie,' Giles drawled insultingly. 'He did a lot more than prosecute you.'

Colour flooded her cheeks and then she went white. 'If you believe that, and Jeremy is supposedly a friend of yours, why are you doing this to him too? And his wife, she's going to be there. Or is that the idea, are you trying to get Glenda Lindsay for yourself?' she scorned.

'Glenda?' Giles snapped suspiciously. 'Why the hell should I want her?'

'Because you——' she broke off, realising she had almost implicated Wanda, and Giles wasn't even aware that she knew her.

'Because . . .?' he prompted.

'You said last night that you're a man, and I know you're a virile one, and Glenda Lindsay is very beautiful, I remember that.'

'So it automatically follows that I want her in my bed?' he rasped.

'Well, doesn't it?'

'No, it damn well doesn't! They're friends of mine, both of them, and that's all.'

'Then you should try choosing better ones, ones that don't lie to you.'

'Why, you——!' He grasped her wrist, twisting her arm behind her back. 'You little bitch! Just because you got caught out it doesn't mean you have to bitch at everyone concerned.'

'I'll bitch at *you* any time I damn well please,' she spat the words at him. 'I hate you!'

'Say that once more and I'll——'

'Hit me?' she taunted.

'No,' he ground out, 'I'll do this!' His mouth came down savagely on hers, pressing her inner lip against her teeth. As he raised his head his eyes gleaming triumphantly down at her. 'Had enough?' he taunted.

'I hate you, I hate you!' she repeated defiantly, her

mouth sore and bruised.

'Don't say I didn't warn you,' he said fiercely, his mouth once more on hers, uncaring of her cry of pain.

The kiss was a punishment, and Leonie didn't enjoy a second of it; her arm twisted painfully, the ragged edge of her sore lip grated against her teeth

'Oh! I—er—I'll come back later. I—er—Excuse me.'

They both looked up to see the door closing behind an embarrassed Emily. Giles pushed Leonie disgustedly away from him.

'Oh, hell!' he swore angrily, running an agitated hand through the thickness of his hair. 'I wish she hadn't seen that.'

'Frightened she might see more in it than your anger and my hate?' Leonie scorned, touching the ragged flesh of her mouth with tentative fingers.

'Oh, get out of here,' he said contemptuously.

'I want to—right out,' she told him vehemently. 'I'm not staying here for your dinner party. You can just get by without me. I'm sure that won't be too difficult.'

'It won't be difficult at all, because you aren't going anywhere.'

'Who says I'm not?' she challenged.

'I do,' he replied calmly.

She gave a scornful laugh. 'And why should what you say make any difference to me?'

His eyes narrowed. 'You really want me to tell you?'

'I'm going out!' She swung away from him.

'You'll stay here!'

'Make me!'

Giles gave a weary sigh. 'You don't really want that. Haven't I hurt you enough for one night?'

'The first minute I saw you you started hurting me,

and you haven't stopped since. Oh, all right, Giles, I'll stay to your dinner party, I'll play your little game for you, but when it's over I'll only hate you more.'

'I think I can stand that. The way you hate I can take as much as you want to give.' His gaze ran over her insultingly, lingering on her denim-clad thighs and the thrust of her breasts beneath the vest top she wore. 'You look about sixteen in that outfit,' he snapped.

'Sorry, sir. I'll change immediately, sir. Black bra and suspender belt to your liking, sir?' she sneered.

He smiled, a genuinely humorous smile, instantly looking younger, the tension leaving his body. 'It's a tantalising thought. Perhaps you could brighten up a winter evening for me that way some time.'

'I won't be here then!'

'You could be. And I think black could be your colour. Do you have a black dress with you?'

She flushed her resentment. As it happened, she did have a black dress, a slinky affair that she had never quite had the nerve to wear. 'I'll wear what I please!' she told him angrily.

'Wear what I please, Leonie. I want you to look beautiful. Not that you don't usually,' he added ruefully. 'Too beautiful on occasion. Even in that outfit you look lovely. So wear the black dress, hmm?'

Her chin was held high. 'I might,' she said grudgingly.

'For me.'

'That's a definite way of making me wear something else!' and with an audacious wrinkling of her nose she left the room.

She put on the black dress as she had known she would, looking sophisticated and very self-assured. If only she felt that way too! Tonight she was to see Jeremy again for the first time in four years. How would she feel about him after all this time? In her mind she hated him, but how would she feel about actually seeing the man himself.

Emily called at her room for her shortly before seven, a slightly embarrassed Emily. 'I'm so sorry, dear,' she rushed into breathless speech, 'I had no idea—Well, I—I didn't realise——'

'It's all right,' Leonie assured her. 'It was only a kiss,' she casually dismissed what had been a savage onslaught, her mouth still slightly swollen from the encounter.

'It looked a little more than that, dear. Are you and Giles——'

'We're just friends, Emily.' Leonie moved jerkily to the door. 'Really, that's all.'

'But—no, I mustn't interfere,' Emily reprimanded herself. 'Giles wouldn't thank me for it.'

There were several people already in the sitting-room when they entered, but a hurried look round revealed that Jeremy and his wife hadn't yet arrived. Giles was talking to a pretty brunette on the other side of the room, although he looked up as Leonie glanced over at him, almost as if he had felt her presence.

Leonie's heart seemed to stop beating, her breath catching in her throat. She loved him! She *loved* Giles Noble. In that moment it all became clear, her initial attraction to him four years ago buried beneath the humiliation she had suffered at his hands.

She hadn't loved him then, couldn't have done, although he had made enough of an impression not to be forgotten. That love had happened since meeting him again, the mindless attraction to him was not just due to sexual excitement after all.

She turned away from him, blotting out the dangerous magnetism of him. No wonder she hadn't been able to run away from him, despite the terrible provocation from him. She couldn't leave him because she loved him, and that love was filling her with such warmth she just wanted to walk across the room and stand next to him, just so that she could be close to him.

'You look sensational.'

Leonie spun round, her face pale as she confronted Giles. She knew every feature of his strong face, knew every hard curve of his body. And now she knew she loved him. 'Thank you,' she said jerkily, breathlessly, completely confused by her own emotions.

'Don't let me down now,' he warned softly.

'Let you down?' she repeated dazedly.

'I saw your reaction to Jeremy,' he told her harshly. 'You went completely white.'

Jeremy! Was he here? 'I——' she bit her lip. She couldn't very well tell Giles she had gone white because of the discovery of her love for *him*! 'Where is he?'

'Don't you know?' he taunted.

'If I did I would hardly be asking!' Her nerves were all strung out, the precariousness of loving a man like Giles all too evident to her.

He gave a sardonic smile. 'He's near the window, talking to my aunt.'

Leonie's gaze swung over in that direction, coldly taking in the fact that Jeremy had changed little since she last saw him. He was still tall and slim, his handsomeness undiminished, a touch of grey among the blond hair at his temples adding distinction. He was chatting easily to Emily, making the elderly woman laugh at his remarks. Yes, he was still as handsome and assured—and he left Leonie cold!

She could now see him for exactly what he was, a middle-aged charmer who preyed on the adoration of naïve teenagers like she had been. Oh, he had surface appeal, but he was shallow, nothing like the god she had thought him to be four years ago. Next to Giles Jeremy was insignificant, merely a good-looking man she could look at objectively. Giles wasn't the cold man she had once thought him, his emotions ran so deep it would take a lifetime to know all his complexities. If only she had a lifetime!

'Come on,' he grasped the top of her arm and began to pull her over to where Jeremy stood.

Leonie hung back. 'Where are you taking me?'

His eyes were cruel. 'To meet a friend of mine.'

'No!'

Giles glowered down at her, a barely leashed violence about him. 'What do you mean, no?'

She was breathing hard. 'I mean exactly that—no. I won't be put through this charade any longer.'

'You'll do what I want you to,' he ground out softly, a pleasant smile on his face for his guests.

'No . . .'

'Yes!'

'Giles, please! I don't want to meet Jeremy again.' Her eyes pleaded with him, but his features remained rigid, unyielding as the man himself. 'Giles, please!'

He seemed to go white, his fingers tightened around her arm. 'Why can't you beg like that when I make love to you?' he groaned, his eyes almost black.

'Giles!' She was conscious of no one but him, both of them seemingly lost in a battle of emotions.

He drew a deep breath. 'You're right, this is hardly the time for this. Let's go and talk to your lover.'

Leonie went with him, mainly because she knew she couldn't fight him in front of this room full of people. They seemed to have attracted more than their fair share of curious glances already, without her causing a scene.

Jeremy turned to smile at them as they approached, the smile not changing at all as his gaze ran appreciatively over Leonie's slender curves. Leonie withstood that look with difficulty, expecting at any moment for him to expose her to the other people here. But he didn't, his smile charming as he looked down at her.

'You must be Leonora Carter,' he said softly. 'Emily has just been telling me about her beautiful assistant. I can see now that she understated rather than overstated.'

He didn't recognise her! Leonie almost choked with relieved laughter. Jeremy didn't even remember her! And why should he? According to Wanda there had been plenty of other women in her father's life since Leonie, plenty of other girls fooled by his practised seduction.

She gave Giles a glance from beneath lowered lashes. His jaw was rigid, his expression giving away none of his inner feelings. She turned back to Jeremy, forcing herself to smile at him. 'Yes, I'm Leonie Carter,' she acknowledged huskily.

'Jeremy Lindsay.' He held out his hand politely.

The touch of his hand meant nothing to her either. Once upon a time she would have trembled even at this casual touch, now it left her cold, and she extricated her hand as soon as she could without seeming impolite.

'Jeremy,' Giles greeted tersely. 'What have you done with your lovely wife?'

As his hand was still on her arm Giles must have felt Leonie tense, but he gave no indication of it. Jeremy might not recognise her with the outward differences in her appearance, but a woman was less likely to be fooled by a change of hairstyle and a more sophisticated way of dressing. She could only hope that Glenda Lindsay had long ago forgotten her—after all, they had never actually met.

'She wasn't able to come with me, I'm afraid. Wanda telephoned at the last minute. Some crisis or other,' he accepted a drink off Davenport, 'that only a mother could deal with.'

Leonie's interest had quickened at the mention of Wanda. It didn't seem at all likely that Wanda would call her mother for help over anything. Unless it was something to do with Phil! She had to find out.

'I hope you'll excuse me for a few minutes.' She gave a dazzling smile, looking at no one in particular, studiously avoiding looking at Giles. 'I—er—I have to make an important telephone call.'

'Who to?' Giles' fingers on her arm refused to be shaken off.

'I—er—I forgot, I arranged to meet someone this evening. I have to let them know I won't be going after all.'

'Use the telephone in my study,' he instructed tightly.

'I—Thank you. Excuse me.' She turned blindly away.

Davenport showed her into the meticulously tidy room, the predominant feature a huge mahogany desk and leather swivel chair. No doubt Giles did a lot of work at home—hadn't he admitted as much when trying to put her off the idea of marrying him?

It felt like sacrilege to be sitting in the comfort of his chair, but she soon forgot about that once she got through to Phil.

'What's the matter?' he asked as soon as he realised who it was.

'Nothing's the matter with me. I just wondered if there was anything wrong your end.'

'Should there be?' He sounded puzzled.

'No. But I—I just had this feeling . . .' She could hardly tell him Jeremy had put the idea in her head!

Phil laughed. 'Feminine intuition? Well, this time it was wrong. Wanda and I were just about to go down to the local for a pint.'

'Wanda's there?'

'She's more or less moved in,' he said ruefully. 'I've tried throwing her out, but she keeps coming back.'

'And I'll keep doing it until he agrees to marry me,' Wanda cut in.

So Wanda hadn't telephoned her mother at all. That either meant Glenda hadn't wanted to come here tonight and Jeremy had made up the excuse, or else Glenda had made that excuse to him herself. Whichever one it was she was at least glad Glenda Lindsay hadn't turned up this evening.

'I think marriage is the only answer, Phil,' she teased her brother.

He sighed. 'I think so too. How would you like to be one of the witnesses?'

'Does that mean you agree?' She was excited for Wanda, could hear the other girl laughing happily as she apparently hugged Phil.

'I agree,' he said defeatedly. 'Although how we'll live . . .'

'Love has a way of making money unimportant,' Leonie told him. 'We'll discuss the wedding arrangements on Saturday, if that's okay with you?'

'Yes, fine. I think Wanda's already started writing out a list of things to be done. At this rate she'll have the wedding arranged *for* Saturday!'

'The sooner the better,' Leonie laughed. 'But a pro-posal through a telephone conversation is hardly romantic, Phil.'

'No, I suppose not,' he agreed. 'I'll get off the phone and do the romantic bit now.'

'Okay,' she smiled, not being able to picture her brother going down on one knee. 'I'll look forward to Saturday.'

The smile was still on her lips as she turned to leave the room. She gasped as she saw Giles standing in the open doorway. 'You startled me!' she accused heatedly.

He came into the room, closing the door behind him, that quiet click telling her of his anger more than if he had slammed the door. 'I thought it would be Philip Trent you called,' he said coldly.

'I—Yes. I don't have many friends in London.' She frowned, his still anger frightening her more than his blazing fury.

'We're ready to go in to dinner now,' he told her icily.

Leonie picked up her black evening bag from the top of the desk. 'I'm sorry if I've kept you waiting.'

'I'm used to it,' he said bitterly.

She flushed, his double meaning not lost on her. 'I'm ready now.' She watched him nervously, not sure of his mood at all.

'I'm always ready where you're concerned.' His eyes never left her lips.

'Giles, please, your guests.'

'Yes,' he sighed, 'my guests. Did it bother you that Jeremy didn't even know you?' he asked suddenly.

This time she was ready for his lawyer's ploy. 'Not in the least,' she said tautly.

'Like hell it didn't!' he snapped viciously. 'It

bothered you so much you ran in here like a frightened rabbit.'

'No! No, that isn't true. I'm glad he didn't recognise me. I only came in here because I had to talk to Phil.'

'I heard,' Giles said grimly. 'We'd better go into dinner now. You and I can talk later.'

It sounded like a threat, so much so that Leonie was a nervous wreck throughout the meal. She even knocked her glass of wine over at one stage, although Davenport dealt with that as deftly as he dealt with everything else.

At least Giles hadn't been cruel enough to seat her next to Jeremy, seating her between the plump and jolly Major Fenton, and the rather henpecked Joe Forsythe, who seemed to blossom away from his friendly but overbearing wife. The conversation of the two men was pleasant, and she could have enjoyed herself—if it weren't for the fact that every time she looked up it was to find Giles' gaze fixed on her broodingly.

Jeremy looked at her a couple of times too, although it was an impersonal gaze, no sign of recognition there. What she would have done if he had recognised her she just didn't know!

They took their coffee into the sitting-room, and several of the men had a brandy too, including Giles. Leonie had watched him through dinner, had seen the way Davenport filled his glass with wine again and again. He didn't seem any the worse for the alcohol he had consumed, but no one could be completely sober after drinking that much. His gaze was even more brooding now, his expression quite unpleasant a couple of times when she looked his way and caught him looking right back at her.

'Leonie!'

She stiffened as Giles called her name across the room, making her the cynosure of all eyes. 'Yes?' she asked calmly, her inner turmoil not apparent.

He put out his hand to her. 'Come here.'

Leonie had been talking to Maggie Forsythe, Joe's bossy wife, and she was very aware of the curious look the other woman gave her. Which wasn't surprising! How dared Giles talk to her like this in front of all these people!

'Leonie?' His mouth was a taut line, a nerve pulsating in the hard line of his jaw.

It was a test of will, a duel, she knew that, but with everyone looking at her she had no choice but to go to him. 'Excuse me,' she smiled at Maggie, and walked unhurriedly over to where Giles stood next to Emily. As a gesture of defiance, an effort to show him he hadn't quite won this battle, she ignored the hand he held out to her. Seconds later she realised her gesture had been a waste of time; his arm passed about her waist, his hand resting possessively beneath her breast. She remained rigid against the hardness of his side, her eyes blazing.

Everyone was still watching this curious interplay between them, Emily with an air of expectation about her. That expectation was soon satisfied.

'I'm glad all of my close friends are here,' Giles raised his voice in tone so that everyone in the room could hear him, 'because I have a special announcement to make.'

Leonie looked up at him sharply, noting that the smile on his lips didn't reach the steel of his eyes.

He looked steadily down at her. 'Leonie has consented to be my wife,' he announced very clearly.

If he hadn't been holding her up she would have fallen down. Had he really said he intended *marrying* her? It would seem so, by the warm congratulations coming their way. She accepted Emily's hug dazedly.

'Just friends, indeed!' Emily snorted disgustedly.

Leonie blushed, unable to answer. 'I—We—I——'

'I understand,' Emily patted her hand. 'You didn't want to ruin the surprise.'

'It's certainly that!' Jeremy had joined them without Leonie being aware of it. 'You were very secretive about your fiancée, Giles,' he teased the other man.

'Wasn't I?' Giles drawled, his hold on Leonie still as firm.

'Is one allowed to kiss the future bride?' Jeremy quirked one eyebrow enquiringly.

Leonie recoiled. She didn't want him to kiss her, the very thought of it nauseated her.

Giles's eyes glittered dangerously, but his expression remained calm. 'Go ahead,' he invited harshly.

She forced herself to accept the touch of Jeremy's lips on hers, tensing as he seemed to linger over the caress. Giles had obviously noticed it too, for his fingers dug painfully into her rib-cage.

In the end she was the one who had to move away, laughing lightly to cover the tension that had suddenly gripped them all. 'I think Giles should have been the first one to kiss me after announcing our engagement. Darling?' Her expression was completely challenging, her lips raised invitingly.

'I'm only too glad to oblige,' he drawled, bending his head to claim a kiss that completely obliterated the touch of Jeremy's mouth on hers. He lingered even longer than Jeremy had, so much so that teasing comments started all around them.

Leonie was starry-eyed by the time he released her, although the malevolent look in Jeremy Lindsay's narrowed blue eyes soon wiped the smile off her face. The expression was quickly gone, so quickly that she thought she must have imagined it. Of course she had imagined it, there was simply no reason for him to look like that.

'Shall I serve the champagne now, sir?' Davenport enquired stiffly.

'Champagne?' Emily echoed excitedly. 'How lovely!'

'Only the best for Giles' fiancée,' Jeremy said smoothly.

'But of course,' Giles agreed curtly.

'Don't you have a ring, Leonie?' Jeremy asked her, looking pointedly at her bare hand, the wedding ring Tom had given her being now locked away in her jewellery box.

'I——'

'Yes, she has a ring,' Giles interrupted. 'It won't be ready until Saturday. It had to be altered.'

'I see,' Jeremy said dryly. 'Well, congratulations, both of you. When is the wedding?'

'Next month,' Giles informed him. 'I've waited long enough for my bride, I don't intend waiting a moment longer than I have to.' His expression was possessive as he looked down at her.

'Glenda will be sorry to have missed meeting your future wife,' Jeremy said thoughtfully. 'I know, you'll both have to come over to dinner one night.' He looked at them enquiringly.

Leonie paled. The last thing she wanted was to meet Jeremy and his wife socially, especially at a dinner party that might only be for the four of them. 'Giles——'

'Perhaps we can arrange something another time, Jeremy,' he responded to her plea. 'Leonie isn't living in London at the moment. Maybe later . . .'

'Yes, of course.'

'Let's all drink a toast,' Emily raised her glass of champagne. 'To Giles and Leonora.'

Leonie withstood the good wishes for the next ten minutes or so, relieved when the conversation once again became general and the limelight was off Giles and herself. 'Why?' she asked him in a fierce whisper.

He didn't even look at her. 'You said you wanted to get married.'

'Yes, but——'

'Not now, Leonie,' he said tautly. 'Wait until our guests have gone, we can—talk then.'

'But they aren't *our* guests, Giles, that's the whole point. You——'

'Not *now*, Leonie.' He turned to glare at her. 'You've got what you wanted, now just shut up.'

'Giles——'

'Leave me alone! Just stay out of my way for the rest of the evening.' He walked off.

'I really must congratulate, you, Mrs Carter,' a familiar voice remarked softly behind her.

She spun to confront Jeremy Lindsay. 'You've already done so, Mr Lindsay,' she smiled to take the sting out of her words.

'So I have.' He twiddled his glass between his fingers. 'But we'd all begun to think—all of Giles' friends, that is—that he was going to escape the net.'

'Maybe he wants to be caught in it.'

'Maybe,' he nodded. 'The bait is certainly attractive enough.'

'Thank you,' she accepted coolly, not liking his insulting tone one little bit.

'Mm,' suddenly his gaze was razor-sharp. 'But then it always was, wasn't it, Leonie?'

If anything she went even whiter, her breath all seeming to have left her body at once, and at a time when she couldn't inhale either. 'I—I'm sorry?' She tried to appear calm, knowing that she failed. 'What do you mean, Mr Lindsay?'

His mouth twisted. 'I mean that you were always attractive, but now you're beautiful. Does Giles know who you are?'

She gave a light laugh. 'What a strange question, Mr Lindsay!' He *knew*—Jeremy knew exactly who she was! Not remembering her had all been a pretence, and he had fooled everyone, including herself. And she hadn't imagined that look on Jeremy's face a few minutes ago when Giles had kissed her, he really had looked at her as if he hated her—or Giles, or both.

Giles was watching them! He acted as if he were listening to Maggie Forsythe, but really he was watching every move she and Jeremy made. He was cold with anger, absolutely rigid with it, and he would never let her get away with talking to Jeremy alone like this, even if she hadn't been the one to instigate the conversation.

'Not so strange, Leonie,' Jeremy drawled at her side. 'Being engaged to marry someone like you could damage his career. His career means everything to him, you know.'

She did know, had always known. 'I'm sorry, Mr Lindsay,' she still tried to bluff her way through this. If she didn't admit to anything then he surely couldn't openly expose her. 'I don't understand what you mean by a woman like me.'

'You know, Leonie,' he scorned. 'You know exactly what I mean.'

'No——'

'Yes! I understand you're staying with Giles' aunt?' His eyes were narrowed.

She frowned her puzzlement. 'I work with her.'

He nodded. 'Very well, I'll be in touch.'

'Oh, but—Jeremy!' She stopped him walking away from her. 'What do you mean to do?' She dropped all pretence, knowing full well that he knew exactly who and what she was.

He shrugged. 'I haven't decided yet. But I'm sure I don't have to impress upon you how important it is that no scandal is attached to Giles?'

'No,' she acknowledged dully. 'But I thought he was a friend of yours?'

'Oh, he is. But I don't even allow friends to walk off with the woman I once wanted—*still* want. Like I said, I'll be in touch.' He tapped her playfully on the cheek.

Leonie turned away, biting her lip as she saw the fury on Giles' face.

CHAPTER SEVEN

'WHAT did he want?' Giles stormed later, after all the guests had left, leaving the two of them alone in the sitting-room. 'What did he say to you?' he demanded to know. 'Tell me, damn you!' He shook her hard.

'I—I'm trying to tell you,' she quavered, feeling dizzy as he continued to shake her. 'He was just congratulating me on my engagement to you,' she told him evasively.

'It didn't take him ten minutes to say that. I want to know, Leonie,' he ordered grimly. 'What did he say?'

She sought desperately about in her mind for a feasible excuse. She couldn't tell him the truth. He wouldn't believe her anyway, not when Jeremy had been so charming the rest of the evening, giving no indication that he had more or less threatened her.

'If you must know, he made a pass at me!' she told Giles now.

He stopped shaking her, his gaze searching her face with thorough intensity. 'Is that the truth?' he asked slowly.

'Yes,' she nodded eagerly, feeling she could be forgiven this small exaggeration. 'Yes, it's true.'

Giles smiled. 'How ironic!'

'Yes. Why did you do it, Giles? Why announce our engagement?'

'Why?' he rasped. 'Because I'm not letting you marry anyone else but me, that's why.'

'Anyone else . . .?' she echoed dazedly.

'I heard you on the telephone to Philip Trent! Good God, girl, you more or less proposed to him! And he accepted. But he isn't getting you,' his face was a livid mask of anger. 'I want you and this time around I'm going to have you, even if I do have to marry you first. You sell yourself very high these days,' he sneered insultingly. 'At one time anyone could have you for the price of a dinner and some wine. Well, I'm upping my bid. I'm sure you realise that as my wife you'll be infinitely more comfortable than you would be married to Philip Trent.'

'But Phil wasn't proposing to *me*,' she protested. 'He——'

'I'm well aware that you brought up the suggestion of marriage,' he said disgustedly. 'But materially I can give you more than he can.'

'And in other ways?'

His mouth twisted. 'In other ways too! Tell me Leonie,' he pulled her hard against him, 'Whose love-making do you prefer, his or mine?' He made no attempt to touch her other than with the hard length of his body, his hands and lips were denied to her. 'Well?' he demanded as she remained silent.

He must be able to feel the way she quivered against him, must know what effect he had on her. 'You don't need me to answer that.' her eyes were on a level with the cleft in his chin, his jaw unyielding. 'You already know the answer.'

'I want to hear you say it.'

'Why? So you can mock me some more? she said angrily. 'Well, I'll marry you, Giles. But the price just went up.' She met his furious gaze unflinchingly.

He flung her away from him as if the touch of her revolted him. 'What more do you want?' he rasped harshly.

'Money.' Her voice was hard.

'How much?' His eyes narrowed.

'How much do you have?'

'Oh no,' his laugh was bitter. 'You tell me how much you think you're worth and I'll tell you whether or not I have that much.'

She thought quickly. Her anger had got her into this situation. If she asked for a completely ridiculous sum he would turn the idea down flat and the whole thing could be forgotten. The figure Phil had mentioned the other day sprang to mind. 'A hundred thousand pounds,' she told him calmly.

She had to admire the way he didn't even flinch, but he didn't laugh either; he seemed to seriously consider the proposal. 'Why a hundred thousand?' he asked thoughtfully. 'Why not a hundred and fifty thousand, or just fifty thousand? Why the specific amount of a hundred thousand?'

Leonie was taken aback by his attitude, surprised he hadn't just dismissed the idea out of hand. She shrugged. 'It seemed a nice round figure.'

'But so is two hundred thousand, or even three hundred thousand. You must know that my family fortune is vast, that even half a million is merely a drop in the ocean?'

'It is?' she gasped.

'You know it is.'

'But I don't! I didn't realise——'

'That I'm a very rich man?' he mocked harshly. 'Liar!'

'But if you're so rich why do you—why do you work?'

'Because I like it. I'm not the type rich playboys are made of. So now you know, do you want to increase the price even more?'

'No! I—You must know I was joking just now about the money. You angered me, I was just trying to shock you.'

'Why a hundred thousand, Leonie?' he persisted. 'It couldn't be for your lover, now could it?'

'Which one?' she asked shrilly. 'You seem to credit me with quite a few.'

Giles' hand went around her wrist, clamping down on her slender bones. 'I could break this as easily as you broke that china figurine,' he threatened savagely.

'I—I'm sorry about that, Emily told me it was one of your favourite pieces.' She groaned softly in her throat at the pressure he was exerting.

He shrugged. 'I did like it, but I would rather have a flesh and blood woman to caress, especially if that woman was you. Have you made any arrangements to meet Jeremy?'

'I——'

'Have you?' he demanded through gritted teeth.

'No.' Although she had no doubt he meant to get in touch with her some time in the near future.

'And you'd better not. I don't know what sort of arrangement you had with your last husband, but I shall want sole rights to your body and time. There will be no scandal attached to my wife's name, no other men in her life. Don't worry, Leonie,' his mouth twisted, 'I'll make sure your time is fully occupied.'

Colour flooded her cheeks as his meaning became clear. 'Giles——'

'You have yet to tell me why Philip Trent needs that money,' he reminded her tautly.

She paled. 'He doesn't need it. At least, he never asked for it. I just thought——'

'So it's a pay-off for him. How many more of your lovers are going to come to me expecting a hand-out?'

'None!' she blazed.

'Okay,' Giles sighed heavily. 'You can have the money.'

'I can?' Her eyes were wide.

'As long as it gets Trent out of your life, yes. And I mean completely out. You can meet him on Saturday as arranged, tell him he can have the money instead of you, and then you're not to see him again.'

Leonie was very white. 'Are you asking me to choose between the two of you?'

'Yes!'

She turned away. If it came to an out-and-out choice between Giles and Phil then she would have to choose Giles, the man she loved. But she shouldn't be made to choose, Giles had no right to ask that of her. 'Isn't that rather a possessive attitude to take?' she choked.

'It may be.' He was unyielding. 'But it's something you'll have to make your mind up to if you become my wife.'

Leonie sighed. 'Giles——'

'Choose!' he ordered grimly.

Her shoulders slumped. 'You know I choose you.'

'I thought you might,' his tone was dry. 'Very well. Tell Trent on Saturday.' He walked to the door.

Leonie watched him with hurt blue eyes. 'Are you going to bed now?'

'It is after twelve, and I have an early case tomorrow.'

Her mouth drooped with disappointment. 'Don't you say goodnight any more?' She so much wanted him to kiss her, had been aching for this reassurance ever since he had told his friends she was to be his wife.

Giles shrugged, making no move to come back to

her. 'Goodnight,' he said coldly, his gaze flickering impersonally over her face. 'What more do you want, Leonie?' he sighed.

'Nothing,' she said tautly.

'Goodnight, then.'

She was alone. Surely it shouldn't be like this. Giles was the man she was going to marry, surely she shouldn't be left feeling quite so desolate?

But at what price she was to be his wife! She was being made to sacrifice the love and company of the man she had always thought of as her brother, and goodness knows what Jeremy would ask of her. And in the end it would probably all be for nothing. She had no idea what Giles' reaction to her physical innocence would be, although she didn't think it would be a very good reaction. He would want to know why she was untouched, would want to know all about Tom. But one thing good would come out of it, he would know once and for all that she had never been with Jeremy or any other man.

'Are you insane?' Phil wanted to know on Saturday, pulling the curtain back at the window to look down at the men crowded in the street below, Giles' Rolls parked in the middle of them. Phil turned back to look at her. 'I take it those reporters are following you?'

'Yes,' Leonie sighed. 'They've been following us the last two days.'

'That's what happens when you agree to marry someone who's almost like royalty,' Phil scorned. 'And I repeat, are you insane? You can't really be serious about marrying Noble.'

'I am.'

'But you can't marry the man just out of a sense of revenge,' he protested angrily, pacing the room. 'You'll be living the rest of your life with him, not just that one night.'

'Phil——'

'You can't put yourself in that position,' he continued to rave. 'He'll destroy you. He——'

'Phil——'

'He'll make your life hell, Leonie,' Phil groaned. 'I can't let you do it.'

'Will you let me talk, please!' she said firmly. 'Thank you,' she said when she had his full attention. 'Phil, I love him. I love him and I want to marry him.'

His mouth fell open. 'Leonie . . .?'

'It's true. I think it's always been true.' She sighed. 'It's the reason I always hated him so much.' She gave a breathless laugh. 'I know how stupid that sounds, but——'

'No,' Phil contradicted heavily, 'it doesn't sound stupid at all. I had similar feelings about Wanda. While I was in prison I told myself, and her, that I hated her, but if she missed a visit or I didn't get a letter from her I just went to pieces. It's like being a drug addict, you know they aren't good for you, but you can't live without them.'

'But Wanda *is* good for you.'

'Yes, she is. She gives me confidence in myself because she has confidence in me. But when I first met her, when she swore she would wait for me, I thought she was just a rich little bitch who was out for a few laughs at my expense. I didn't answer any of her letters at first, but after a year or so I decided to let her visit me. As soon as I saw her again I knew I had to have her for my wife, and crazy child that she is, she seems to want that too.'

'Because I love you,' she said quietly from behind them.

'Hello, love,' Phil went over to kiss her. 'We have a celebrity in our midst.'

'Is that what all the reporters are about downstairs?'

'Wanda——' Leonie said sharply. 'Wanda, did Giles see you come up here?'

The other girl frowned. 'Is that his car down there? No, I don't think he saw me, there were reporters all around the car.'

'Wrong,' drawled a coldly familiar voice, 'I saw you, Wanda.' Giles entered the room, his gaze contemptuous as he looked from Leonie to Phil, and then back again. 'The plot thickens,' he said slowly.

Leonie's face was stricken. She had asked Giles if she might talk to Phil alone, and after much argument he had agreed. And now this! Looking at it from Giles' point of view the situation looked very suspicious, very suspicious indeed.

'Giles——'

'Let me work this out for myself, Leonie,' he told her coldly. 'My God, you and your brother really went to town on us, didn't you,' he said scornfully. 'Do your parents know about this, Wanda?'

'No. But——'

'I didn't think they would. Do you have any idea what your—involvement with this man would mean to them?' he demanded.

'Yes. But——'

'You don't care,' he finished contemptuously. 'Are you so besotted with him that you don't owe your parents any loyalty?'

'Loyalty!' Wanda echoed angrily. 'The same sort of loyalty they give me? The same sort of loyalty my father gave Leonie when you and he publically humili-ated her?'

'Wanda!' Leonie gasped, looking worriedly at Giles.

'I'm sorry,' Wanda sighed. 'But it's about time Giles was told some home truths about my father. You see, he——'

'You'll have to forgive her,' Leonie cut in hastily. 'She's a little overwrought.'

'And you?' Giles snapped angrily. 'What's your excuse for your affection for this man? Don't bother to answer, I can guess. Well, in future, Trent, you can stay away from Leonie. Wanda's old enough to make her own mind up about the friends she keeps, but Leonie is now my property. Here,' he threw a cheque down on to the table, 'that's payment for her.'

'Why, you——'

Leonie restrained her brother with an effort. 'It's all right, Phil,' she soothed. 'Now just calm down.'

'But that bastard——'

'Just gave you the money you need,' she said warningly. 'And I want you to take it.'

'But, Leonie——'

'Take it, Phil. And use it. I told you earlier, this is what I want. And I want you to have what you want too. After all,' she added bitterly, 'Giles is rich enough, aren't you, darling?' Her voice was icy.

'Let's get out of here,' he snapped. 'And if you had any sense, Wanda, you'd get out too.'

'I think the only person in this room without sense is you, Giles,' she told him rudely. 'Can't you see what sort of person Leonie is?'

His mouth twisted, his eyes bleak. 'I know exactly what sort of person she is. If you aren't down at the car within two minutes, Leonie, I'll come back up here and get you.' He slammed out of the room.

'My God!' Phil gasped. 'You can't marry him, Leonie. The man's insane!'

She shrugged resignedly. 'He has his—nicer moments.'

'He's insane with *jealousy*, Leonie,' Phil said disbelievingly. 'Why on earth should he be jealous of *me*?'

'He just is,' she evaded. 'Don't worry, he's the same about every man I come into contact with. Look, I have to go. But take the money, I want you to have it for your restaurant.'

Wanda had picked up the cheque, looking down at it. 'He can't mean this,' she said dazedly. 'A hundred thousand pounds!'

'Let me see,' Phil took it from her. 'Is he joking?' he asked Leonie.

'Did he look in a humorous mood?' she taunted. 'It's the amount I asked for.'

'You—Leonie, what have you been up to?'

'Exactly what Giles told you I'd done—sold myself. Don't you think he deserves it?'

'He may do, but I don't think you do.'

'I have to go,' she said worriedly. 'But, Phil, he—he meant it about staying away from me.' She bit her lip. 'I—I'm sorry.'

'Do you mean——'

'I have to go,' she repeated with a hurried glance at her wristwatch. 'Good—good luck with the wedding.' Tears were streaming down her face.

'Leonie——'

'No Phil,' Wanda stopped him. 'I chose you over my family rather than risk losing you, now Leonie is doing the same thing for Giles. Be happy, Leonie,' she told her gently.

'How can she be happy with him?' Phil said disgustedly.

'Phil!' his fiancée warned. 'He's going to be your sister's husband, and she loves him.'

Leonie ran out of the room, unable to bear it any more. She had to face a barrage of cameras and reporters once she got outside the building. Giles moved swiftly to open the car door for her, causing the attention to transfer to him.

'When's the wedding, Mr Noble?'

'How long have you known each other?'

'Does Mrs Carter have any children from her previous marriage?'

The last question caused Giles to spin round and face his questioner. His expression remained bland with effort. 'No, my fiancée does not have any children. Now would you all stop following us. I gave you a press release yesterday, I have nothing to add to that.'

Leonie hadn't known of his contact with the newspapers, and the shock of seeing a picture of herself and Giles on the front page of more than one newspaper this morning had rendered her speechless. Emily had been overjoyed, in fact they seemed to be surrounded by a glow of satisfaction. The fact that her nephew and Leonie didn't exactly act like lovers did not seem to have been noticed by her. She was full of plans for the wedding, most of which only needed Leonie's smiling approval.

'Why didn't you have any children?' Giles suddenly asked her, once the press had been left far behind them.

'I—Because we—I——' She didn't know what to say, her face was bright red with embarrassment.

'Don't children figure in your plans for the rest of your life?' Giles rasped.

'I—I haven't thought about it. Do you want children?' The thought of a dark-haired baby who looked like Giles snuggled up to her breast gave her a warm glow. How lovely to be the mother of Giles' children!

'I haven't thought about it either. I suppose in time
...'

'Yes,' she agreed dully. He didn't want her to have
his child! She knew it as surely as if he had uttered the
cruel words of rejection. 'Giles, are you expecting our
marriage to last?' she asked bravely.

His dark head went back proudly. 'Aren't you?'

'I asked first.'

He shrugged. 'No one can guarantee the success of a
marriage.'

'Your parents weren't happy together, were they?'

'No.'

He was very uncommunicative, but that didn't put
her off. 'Do you think we'll be happy?'

'I doubt it,' he said coldly. 'You're very like my
mother. She was a social butterfly, one man wasn't
enough for her. My father was a broken man before
she left him.'

'Well, at least you won't suffer that fate,' Leonie
said bitterly. 'You don't love me, so I doubt it will
even dent your armour when I leave.'

'Shouldn't you at least wait until after the wedding
before talking of leaving me?' Giles derided.

'Are you sure you really want there to be a wedding?
After all, you only really made that announcement
because you thought I was going to marry Phil.'

'You're marrying me,' he told her abruptly. 'And
Wanda is going to marry Philip Trent, isn't she?'

Leonie looked down at her hands. 'Yes.'

'So it's all worked out to your advantage, hasn't it?'
he probed.

'If you say so.'

'You don't sound too sure.'

She wasn't sure about anything. The only time she
felt close to Giles was when he held her in his arms

and made love to her, something he hadn't felt inclined to do since the night of the dinner party. He never touched her unless he could help it.

'Leonie!' he prompted harshly.

'Sorry,' she shook herself out of her dream world. 'Yes, it's all worked out well. Where are we going, Giles?' She noticed they were driving into town and not away from it towards Giles' home.

'To pick up your ring, where else?' He miraculously appeared to have found a parking space, and reversed the Rolls into it.

Her eyes widened. 'You mean there really is a ring?'

'Of course.'

'When did you buy it?' she frowned.

'I didn't. It's a family heirloom. It had to be made smaller so that it would fit you. Your other ring, where is it?'

'My wedding ring?'

'Yes!'

'I—I took it off. It's in my jewellery box.'

'That saves me the trouble of taking it off myself,' he rasped. He turned to look out of the window. 'Did you love him?'

'Tom?'

'If that was your husband's name, yes,' he said rigidly.

'Yes, I loved him. He was——'

'I don't want to know!' he snapped harshly, swinging out of the car. 'Let's get this over with. My aunt is waiting to see the Noble ring on your finger.'

It was a beautiful ring, a cluster of diamonds that weighed heavily on her finger. Emily was ecstatic when she saw Leonie was wearing it, her excited chatter making Giles retreat to his study on the excuse of urgent work.

'When you're married you'll have to put a stop to that,' Emily tutted. 'He works much too hard.'

'And you think I could stop him?' Leonie scorned.

'Of course you could, dear.' Emily gave a coy smile. 'A wife has a way of doing these things, a way no other woman who's been in a man's life can.'

'Why, Emily,' she teased, 'did you manage your husband like that?'

'Frank never needed managing. He was the kindest, most thoughtful—Well, he was a good husband. But Giles is thirty-nine, a little old to be thinking of changing his solitary way of life. Not that I don't think he'll make a wonderful husband, I'm sure he will, it just may take a little time, that's all.'

Leonie smiled. 'Are you warning me, Emily?'

'Of course not, Leonora,' she said indignantly. 'It's just that I know Giles can be a—well, a little difficult. He's had his own way for so long now, I suppose it will take him a little time to adjust to being married. Do you plan to have children? Silly of me to ask,' she blushed. 'It's a bit soon for you to have discussed it.'

'Actually we have, but only generally.'

'I'd like it if you had children,' Emily said dreamily. 'Frank and I didn't have any of our own, so any children you and Giles have will be the nearest thing I'll ever have to grandchildren.'

'We'll try to oblige,' Leonie teased.

'Giles will make a wonderful father.'

He would too. He would be strict, but it would be a case of the iron fist in a velvet glove. You always knew where you stood with Giles, and any child of his would be totally secure in his love.

Phil telephoned her several times over the weekend, but somehow Giles always intercepted the calls before Leonie found out about them. He took great pleasure in telling her about them before he parted from her and Emily on Sunday evening. Emily had tactfully retired to her room soon after they returned to Rose Cottage, and was probably even now envisaging them in each other's arms. Instead of which they were like cold strangers.

'If Trent telephones you here,' Giles told her coldly, 'I want you to refuse to speak to him.'

'I can't do that,' she protested.

His eyes narrowed dangerously. 'Do you want me to prove once again that you belong to me?'

Her head went back challengingly. 'Yes, I think I do. I think I might quite like that.' He hadn't kissed her since Wednesday, and she was hungry for him.

His look was contemptuous as he pulled her towards him. 'You wanton little bitch!' His mouth ground down on hers.

He was insulting her again, telling her with his mouth the low opinion he had of her. 'No, Giles!' She wrenched away from him, her eyes dark blue in her pain. 'Please, stop it!'

'What's the matter?' he taunted savagely. 'Isn't that the way you like to be loved? What do you like, Leonie? Do you like this?' His hand was probing beneath her blouse, releasing the single fastening to her bra. 'Do you like this?' His hand cupped her breast. 'And this?' His thumb ran lightly over her nipple.

Leonie swallowed hard, the tears threatening to flood and overflow her eyes. 'You're making me look cheap, Giles. You're deliberately making me look like—like——'

'Like the wanton you are,' he accused viciously. 'Okay, Leonie, if you can't wait until we're married we'll make love now, right here. If you like sex that much then I'd better make sure you get what you want.' He was unbuttoning his shirt, still managing to hold on to her with the other hand. When his shirt was completely undone he pushed her hands beneath the material against his bare chest. 'Make love to me like you did last time,' he invited. 'Give me the benefit of your vast experience.'

'Giles, please . . .'

'Make love to me, Leonie.' He pulled her down on to the sofa. 'Show me how you give a man pleasure.'

She felt so cold, her emotions numb. What Giles had done to her four years ago was nothing to the destruction he was causing now. 'I think after all that I'd rather wait,' she said dully.

'And if I wouldn't?' he rasped, breathing heavily.

'You may not want to, but you will,' she said with certainty. 'I can't believe you would ever use force on a woman.' She didn't think that in the past he had ever needed to!

'I may make you the exception,' he told her grimly. 'After all, why should I deny myself any longer? You're willing—at least, your body is, and I'm more than ready to make love to you.'

'Your aunt is upstairs,' she told him coldly. 'Would you like her to come downstairs and find us—like that?'

'You know I wouldn't.' He moved back to look down at her with contempt. 'What is it about you that makes me want you?' He sounded disgusted with himself.

'Revenge?'

'That's your province.' His mouth twisted, and he rebuttoned his shirt. 'You and Trent really have this situation tied up. Wanda is obviously infatuated with him.'

'She loves him,' Leonie corrected. 'Something you would know nothing about,' she added bitterly.

'And I suppose you do?' He pulled on his jacket.

'Yes!' her tone was vehement.

'Well, in future you can save all the love you're capable of for me.'

'You expect me to love you after the way you treat me?' she gasped.

Giles smiled. 'You aren't capable of the sort of love I want, if you were maybe I wouldn't treat you this way.'

'And maybe you would,' she said resignedly.

He shrugged. 'I doubt it. I'll leave it to you and Emily to arrange the minor details of the wedding. I'll deal with the licence and day. In three weeks' time you'll be my wife.'

'If Jeremy had recognised me would you still want to marry me?' She thought she already knew the answer to that, but she had to be sure.

'No way,' he confirmed. 'I don't want the whole world to know I've been stupid enough to marry a woman who isn't above blackmail to achieve her ends.'

She had known what his answer would be. If Jeremy had told Giles he knew her to be Leonie Gordon then Giles wouldn't even contemplate making her his wife. She had been hesitating about whether or not she should tell Giles that Jeremy hadn't been fooled at all. But now she knew she couldn't do that, not unless she wanted to lose Giles this very minute.

His gaze was insolently appraising. 'If I'd been as intimate with you as Jeremy has been I doubt I would have had the same lapse of memory.'

'I suppose you remember every woman you've ever slept with,' she scorned.

'Vividly,' he drawled.

'Including Sonja Johnson?'

His eyes narrowed to steely slits. 'Sonja and I were together for over a year, of course I remember her.'

'*Were* together?' Leonie echoed. A year! A whole year Sonja Johnson had been in his life. A deep aching jealousy racked her body.

'Sonja and I are finished,' he said coldly.

'Does she know that? Or can I expect to have you sneaking off to be with her after we're married?'

'Sonja knows. And I won't be *sneaking* off to anyone. And neither will you, not unless you want to be beaten within an inch of your life.'

'You'd hit me?' she squeaked.

He nodded. 'If I had to. My father was a fool, he let my mother get away with treating him like one too. But I'm far from being a fool, Leonie, so there'll be no other man for you. None. You understand?'

'Yes.'

Oh God, if he should find out about Jeremy!

CHAPTER EIGHT

By the time Jeremy telephoned her she was just
relieved to hear from him at last. Almost a week had
gone by and he hadn't contacted her, a week when she
had waited in dread to hear from him. The relief of his
telephone call was welcome, his request that she meet
him was not.

'I can't, Jeremy. You know I can't,' she pleaded with
him.

'You know you'd better,' he replied smoothly, well
aware that he had all the aces.

'Jeremy——'

'I mean it, Leonie. Come up to London on Saturday
and we can——'

'Not Saturday,' she instantly refused, her voice low.
The telephone was out in the hallway, and Emily or
Dorothy could walk through at any time. The fact that
this call wasn't from Giles was bound to be cause for
speculation. They could probably think it was Phil,
and if Giles should even suspect she had spoke to *him*,
let alone Jeremy . . . 'Giles will be here for the weekend,' she explained.

'Ah yes, Giles. I'm longing to know how the two of
you met up again. How *did* that happen?' he asked
with mocking humour.

'Mind your own damned business!'

'My, my, now you've really aroused my curiosity.
Okay, we'll meet tomorrow as Saturday is out.'

'Tomorrow?' she echoed in a squeaky voice. 'I can't
possibly——'

'For lunch,' Jeremy continued as if she hadn't spoken. 'We can meet in town and then go on to eat.'

'Won't that upset your appointments?' She sought for an excuse not to see him. 'After all, you are a famous Harley Street doctor,' she reminded bitterly.

'I don't have any appointments after lunch tomorrow,' he drawled.

'And I was led to believe you were much in demand,' Leonie taunted sarcastically.

'Oh, I am. I just made sure I kept tomorrow free. I had a feeling Saturday would be out.'

'Why do we have to meet at all, Jeremy? Surely we——' she was cut off by his mocking laughter. 'What's so funny?' she asked tautly.

'You are. You know damn well why we have to meet, we have some unfinished business to sort out.'

'Unfinished——! If you mean what I think you do then I——'

'Leonora,' Emily appeared out of the lounge, a worried frown to her brow. 'Is there anything wrong?'

'I was shouting because I'm talking to a rather aged aunt of mine,' Leonie frantically thought of any excuse that she could. 'I'm trying to invite her to the wedding, but as she's a little deaf . . .'

'Oh, dear,' Emily chuckled. 'Well, good luck.' She went back into the lounge, already lost in her work by the faraway expression in her eyes.

'Your "aged aunt" will meet you outside the Ritz tomorrow at twelve-thirty,' Jeremy told her mockingly. 'Don't be late. I would hate to have to find myself another dining companion—Giles, for instance.'

'Jeremy——' He had already rung off!

She would have to go now. If he should go and see Giles——!

'Everything all right, dear?' Emily looked up from

her notepad as Leonie entered the room. 'Did you get your aunt to understand in the end?'

'Oh—oh yes, I think so.' She gave a nervous smile. 'I—er—I arranged to meet her in town tomorrow so that I could explain it better.'

'That will be nice, dear. Maybe you'll have time to visit Giles in the afternoon. You could get a lift back with him, he's coming up tomorrow evening, isn't he.'

'Oh yes, yes, he is. But I—I think I'll come straight back after lunch, I have some sketches I want to finish before Giles arrives, so that I have the weekend free. Besides, I'll have my car there.'

By twelve-thirty the next day she was beginning to wish she had come by train. There wasn't a parking space to be had anywhere, and the later she was the less likely it was that Jeremy would still be waiting for her. She finally found a space, almost running to the Ritz, causing a few raised eyebrows as she exploded into the quietly exclusive atmosphere of this top London hotel and restaurant.

'Can I help you, madam?' one of the stiff waiters asked politely.

Leonie gathered her scattered wits together, aware that her smart silky suit, long legs in sheer tights, the same legs shown to advantage by the high heels on her sandals, were in complete variance with her harassed expression. If only Jeremy was still here!

'Mr Lindsay,' she said breathlessly. 'I'm supposed to be meeting him here.'

At once the stiffness left his manner, his smile quite jovial. 'Of course, madam. Mr Lindsay told me to expect you. If you would like to come this way?'

She was taken into the lounge, thanking the waiter as she saw Jeremy sitting at a corner table.

'Leonie,' he rose to his feet as she joined him. 'I'm

so glad you could make it.'

She gave him a resentful glance as they both sat down. 'You know I had no choice.'

'You had a choice, Leonie,' he said confidently.

'God, I hate you!' she muttered. He had no right to sit there looking so handsome and assured when he had the power to wreck her fragile happiness with a few cruel words to Giles.

'That's a shame.' He picked up her left hand, looking at her engagement ring. 'Pretty. Yes, it's a pity that you hate me, Leonie. You see, I still find you very desirable.'

She snatched her hand away, rubbing it down her skirt as if the touch of him had contaminated her. 'What do you want from me?'

'What do you think I want?' he rasped, not having missed her gesture. 'Don't be silly, Leonie, you aren't that naïve.'

'But I——'

'Let's go in to lunch first. We can talk after we've eaten.'

'I'd rather talk now,' she insisted stubbornly.

'You'll find I'm much more—amenable when I've eaten,' he drawled. 'Much more willing to listen.'

They ate in the Grill Room, and Leonie admired the ornate gold ceiling and walls as Jeremy gave their order. He didn't even need to ask her what she wanted, knowing her preferences from when they had gone out together. After all, they had dated for about six months before she found out about his married status. He ordered them both melon, poached salmon and salad.

'I trust you still have the same tastes?' he smiled.

'Only in food,' she replied pointedly.

He gave a husky laugh. 'Not in men, hmm, Leonie?'

'Definitely not,' she shuddered.

'I think you more than proved that. Giles is hardly your usual type.'

'Do I have a type?'

'I thought so. What was your husband like?'

'If one more person asks that——!' She gave an angry sigh.

'Giles was curious too, hmm?'

'Leave Giles out of this!'

'Oh, I can't do that, Giles is very much in this. Wednesday was a test, wasn't it?' he mused. 'And you passed with flying colours—with a lot of help from me. You certainly wouldn't be wearing that ring now if I'd decided to tell all Giles' friends about you. Giles is a really good friend, very liberated, until it comes to his own women. About six months ago I tried it on with his latest——'

'Sonja Johnson,' Leonie said bitterly. It had to be her, Giles had admitted that the other woman had been in his life at least a year.

'That's the one,' Jeremy nodded. 'Hey,' he grinned, 'he didn't tell you about her? My God, he did!' he laughed outright now. 'Thanks,' he spoke to the waiter who had brought their melon. 'So Giles has come clean about his past.' His eyes narrowed. 'Did you do the same?'

Leonie's expression was challenging. 'And if I have?'

'Giles would never believe you, especially now.'

'Why especially now?' she asked sharply.

'Well, you've had a husband, and no doubt numerous other men. It would be a bit difficult to act the innocent now,' Jeremy derided.

If only he knew, she thought bitterly. Why was it that both he and Giles presumed she had the morals of an alley-cat?

'Giles is very possessive about his women,' Jeremy

mused. 'He wouldn't let me near Sonja. Still, no doubt she's up for grabs now. Maybe I should give her a call.'

Leonie spiked one of the cubes of melon on her plate. 'I doubt if Giles would feel any differently about your involvement with her,' she said dully.

'You mean he and she——? Well, well,' he smiled. 'I didn't know he had the time for two women in his life, especially two like you.'

'Well, now you know.' She looked at him unflinchingly, once again wondering what she had ever seen in him. There was a weakness about him that she hadn't been aware of before, and she knew he possessed none of Giles' strength of character.

She sat back as the waiter removed their plates, only to put their salmon in front of them seconds later. It surprised her how well Jeremy had remembered the food she liked, sure that there had been many other women in his life.

They ate in silence for several minutes, the wine Jeremy had chosen to go with the meal excellent as usual. Jeremy was an expert on wines, and his knowledge of them had greatly impressed the naïve eighteen-year-old she had once been.

She refused a sweet, although she had to sit and wait to leave while Jeremy ate his cheese. He suggested they have their coffee in the lounge, and she readily agreed, anxious to escape the attentions of the three waiters who had served their meal.

'Shall we get to the point of this meeting?' she suggested tersely once they were in the lounge.

Jeremy sat back, completely relaxed. 'You already know what I want—and that's you.'

She paled, her worst fears realised. 'Me?'

'That's right.' His hand covered hers as it lay on the

sofa beside him, his fingers tightening as she would have moved away. 'I was in love with you four years ago, Leonie.' His tone was deadly serious now.

'You had a funny way of showing it,' she scorned.

'You shouldn't have tried that trick on me. If you'd been just a little more patient you would have been my wife. Oh, yes,' he insisted hardly, 'I was going to divorce Glenda for you.'

Her eyes were wide. 'You would have *married* me?'

'Yes,' he admitted harshly, all the boyish surface charm erased. 'I was mad about you. You wouldn't agree to the relationship I wanted, so I was going to marry you. When I saw you at Giles' flat the other night I thought I was finally going to get a second chance with you. And then he announced your engagement to him!'

'Jeremy, I——'

'But I'm going to have you, Leonie,' he went on savagely. 'I'm sick and tired of seeing a pair of accusing blue eyes in my mind whenever I think of you.'

She was only half listening to him, having been aware of being observed the last few minutes. There was a woman sitting a few feet away from them, and she had been watching them with an interest that Leonie found unnerving.

She was a woman in her late fifties, possibly early sixties, her hair obviously kept that golden blonde colour by the expertise of her hairdresser, her face agelessly beautiful, her eyes blue or grey, it was hard to tell from this distance, her figure slender in the fitted blue dress she wore. She was a very attractive woman, and the man seated with her obviously thought so too, although at the moment he was having trouble holding her attention, and her gaze was more often then not on Jeremy and Leonie.

'Leonie!' Jeremy's voice was sharp.

'Sorry,' she dragged her attention back to him with effort. 'An admirer of yours?'

He followed her line of vision, turning back with a shake of his head. 'Afraid not. Very attractive, though.'

Leonie sighed, the woman now forgotten. 'What's the matter with you, Jeremy? Why can't you stay with one woman?'

'I intended to,' he said sharply, 'but you got away from me.'

'I didn't mean me,' she snapped impatiently. 'Your wife is very beautiful, and you have a lovely daughter too. Why couldn't you have tried to make that a happy marriage?'

'I tried to, in the beginning. Unfortunately Glenda is one of those liberated women who believe in freedom in marriage, and I wasn't going to sit at home waiting for her to come home from her latest lover.'

'You could have divorced her years ago, married someone who didn't have those views on marriage.'

'I told you, I was going to. And now Giles has claimed you,' he said bitterly, standing up to pull her to her feet by the hold he still had on her hand. 'Let's get out of here. We can go to my flat and talk.'

Leonie hung back. 'Not the same flat you told Giles I visited in the past?'

'The same.' He gave a tight smile, his hand under her elbow propelling her out of the hotel and into a passing taxi. 'I want to be alone with you,' he told her, regardless of the listening taxi-driver.

She shook her head. 'No, Jeremy, I—I don't have the time right now. I told Emily I would be back early. And—and Giles is coming down this evening. You're supposed to be my aged aunt, remember,' she added

desperately. 'She would hardly spend the afternoon
dashing around the shops, which is what I would have
to tell Emily I'd been doing.'

Jeremy's eyes were narrowed to icy blue slits. 'Is
that the only reason you've refused?'

She looked down at her hands. 'I'm in love with
Giles, you know.'

'Yes,' it came out as a hiss.

'Don't you care that I'm not in love with you?'

'Of course I damn well care! But I'm willing to take
what I can get. I don't suppose you would consider
marrying me instead of Giles?'

'After your divorce?' she asked bitterly, aware that
the taxi-driver must be listening to every word—and
wondering exactly what he was listening to!

'Would you, Leonie?'

'No, I wouldn't!' she told him indignantly. 'I'm in
love with Giles.'

'Four years ago you were in love with me,' he
reminded her angrily.

'We all have moments of madness,' Leonie derided
coldly.

His mouth tightened fiercely. 'You little bitch! All
right, you won't marry me, but you will come back up
to town one day next week and meet me at the flat. I
insist, Leonie,' he said as she started to protest. 'You
do want your wedding to take place, don't you?' he
added threateningly.

She wasn't sure any more, the price of being Giles'
wife seemed to be very high. Ridiculed by the man she
loved, threatened by a man she didn't love. She was
beginning to wonder if it was worth it, especially as
Giles could throw her out of his life the day after the
wedding.

'Call me one day next week,' she evaded. 'We'll

arrange something then.'

'You mean that?'

'I don't lie, unlike some people. I'm perfectly well
aware of all the lies you told Giles about me.'

'And he believed every word.' Jeremy smiled his
pleasure.

'You made sure he did. Stop the taxi here,' she
touched the driver's shoulder, opening her car door.
'I'll see you next week, Jeremy,' she told him coldly.
'The—gentleman will pay,' she spoke to the driver
before hurrying away to find her car.

'Giles called while you were out,' Emily told her as
soon as she entered the cottage.

Leonie bit her lip. 'Did he say what he wanted?'

'Just to talk to you dear,' Emily told her absently, 'I
told him you were visiting an aunt.'

She went up to her room. Giles would no doubt
question her when they met tonight. She was right, he
did, not even saying hello before he started questioning
her.

'I didn't even know you had an aunt.' He eyed her
with open suspicion.

'Well, now you know I have.' She evaded the intensity of his gaze. 'Would you like a drink?' She moved
to the drinks trolley.

'Whisky, straight.' He took the glass from her, looking very attractive in dark blue shirt and light blue
suit. 'Tell me about her,' he ordered abruptly.

'She's an old lady, a deaf old lady. Now aren't you
going to kiss me hello?'

His mouth twisted. 'You saw Trent in London!
After all that I told you——'

'No, no, I didn't,' she was able to answer honestly.
'Please believe me, Giles, I didn't see Phil.' But she
had been tempted, oh, so tempted.

He continued to look at her for several minutes longer. Finally he shrugged. 'Okay, so you didn't see him. Will your aunt be coming to the wedding?'

Leonie heaved an inward sigh of relief. 'No, she—she can't make it. But she sends her best wishes. I—Will I be allowed to invite Phil to the wedding?'

'No. It's going to be a very quiet affair, only close family——'

'Phil *is* my close family,' she interrupted.

'Too damned close!' Giles growled, scowling heavily. 'I don't want him there.'

'Well, I do. He——'

'Isn't it enough that one of your ex-lovers will be present? Do we have to invite the whole damn lot of them?'

'I want Phil there,' she said stubbornly.

'If he comes he'll bring Wanda, and I wouldn't guarantee peace and harmony when Phil and Wanda meet up with Glenda and Jeremy.'

Leonie swallowed hard. 'You're inviting Jeremy?'

'What other ex-lover did you think I had in mind?' He glared.

'I don't know,' she cried. 'Oh, Giles, why are you always so grim? Don't you ever smile? Can't you ever be happy?'

His glass landed on the table with a clatter. 'I'm so tied up in knots about you I'm surprised I can even speak.' He was breathing hard. 'I've missed you this week, the house seems empty without you.'

Leonie blushed, a smile of pleasure lighting up her strained features. 'That's nice,' she said huskily.

'Not for me it isn't,' he sighed. 'You're on my mind day and night. You may find that funny, but——'

'Not funny, Giles,' she denied instantly, moving so that she was standing only a few inches away from him, her hands resting lightly on his chest. 'Never funny. I've been having sleepless nights myself.'

His eyebrows rose. 'Over me?'

'Of course over you.' Her laugh caught in her throat, her expression chiding. 'I—I want you,' she gulped at the enormity of her admission. 'I've missed you too, darling.'

'I didn't know endearments came with the deal,' he murmured before his mouth closed gently over hers.

It was an undemanding kiss, an asking where before there had only ever been taking. It was a kiss given without passion, just a gentle caress that made Leonie feel closer to him than if they had actually made love. She had the answer to her earlier question, moments like this made marrying Giles worth any amount of insults and suffering.

Giles leant his forehead on hers. 'You're everything a woman should be,' he said shakily. 'Beautiful to look at, fun to be with, sometimes childishly innocent and at other times completely uninhibited. Making love to you should prove quite an experience.'

Leonie bit her bottom lip. 'I—er—What if I don't satisfy you?' She looked at him anxiously.

His eyes narrowed. 'Are you offering me a trial run?'

'No! I just thought——'

'I didn't think you would be.' He moved away from her. 'I might not bother to marry you then, might I?'

'I didn't mean that,' she gasped, knowing their gentle moment together had passed—for the moment.

'Of course you did.' He poured himself some more whisky, swallowing it down in one gulp. 'God, I'm drinking too much,' he put the glass down with an expression of self-disgust. 'I hardly ever used to drink before we met again.'

'Then you mustn't drink now. You shouldn't endanger your career in this way.'

The laugh he gave was bitter. 'So you see yourself as a prominent barrister's wife after all,' he scorned.

'Jeremy said——'

'Jeremy?' His face was black with a dangerous anger, his fingers squeezing painfully into her arm. 'When did you see Jeremy? Today? Did you see him today?'

His anger was barely leashed and Leonie knew it. 'He mentioned at the dinner party that your career is important to you.'

'When did he *mention* it?'

'Just before he made that pass at me. I told you about that.'

'So you did,' he agreed tautly.

'Giles, can't I invite Phil to the wedding?' She had to get his attention away from Jeremy. Goodness, what a slip that had been! She would have to be more careful what she said.

'No, you can't. But while we're on the subject of him, he hasn't cashed that cheque.'

Leonie frowned. 'He hasn't?'

'No,' Giles shook his head. 'I warned my bank about it, as it was such a large amount. But so far they've heard nothing.'

It was Phil being proud again. She should have known he wouldn't accept the money. I'll have to see him——'

'No!' he instantly cut in. 'And you won't telephone him either. I'll deal with it myself.'

Her eyes widened. 'You'll go and see him?'

'I'll deal with it.' His expression was remote. 'By the way, we have a dinner invitation.'

'We do?'

'Mm. Glenda has invited us to dinner on Wednesday.'

Leonie gulped. 'Glenda Lindsay?'

'That's right.'

'But I—You didn't accept, did you?' Oh God, she hoped not! And Jeremy hadn't mentioned this invitation at lunchtime, although as it came from his wife perhaps he didn't know about it yet.

'I did,' Giles told her arrogantly. 'They happen to be my friends.'

'Yes, but surely——'

'We're going, Leonie. You can come up to town in the afternoon. I'll tell Davenport to expect you.'

'Giles, please——'

His face was stony. 'Don't argue with me, Leonie.'

'Why the hell shouldn't I?' She lost her temper, tired of his domineering attitude. 'I don't want to go to dinner with the Lindsays. And I think I should be allowed some say in what we do. If you wanted a complacent wife then perhaps you should have chosen someone else.'

'Finished?' he raised his eyebrows mockingly. 'Good. I don't remember there being any question of choice where you're concerned, I just need to have you. But I don't expect to give up my friends when I marry you.'

'I didn't expect to have to give up my family, but you made me.' she reminded him bitterly.

'The only person I've made you give up is Philip Trent.'

'Exactly, my family. And if you count Jeremy as a friend then I hate to think what your enemies are like.' There were two spots of bright colour high in her cheeks. 'He doesn't give a damn about your friendship. He just uses people, as he's using——'

'Yes?' Giles prompted. 'Using . . .?'

'You,' she made up. 'He didn't care that you'd just announced our engagement when he made that pass at me last week.'

To her chagrin Giles only smiled. 'Jeremy makes a pass at every woman he comes into contact with. He wouldn't be Jeremy if he didn't.'

'And that excuses him?' Leonie asked shrilly.

'It proves you aren't any different to him than any other woman he meets. If he had ignored how beautiful you are then I would have been suspicious.'

Clever, clever Jeremy. How well he knew Giles—and how little Giles knew Jeremy!

The question of going to the Lindsay's was dropped as Emily joined them for dinner. Leonie noticed that the older woman seemed nervy, her sentences disjointed, her eyes fever-bright. There was something wrong with Emily, and it was obvious to anyone who knew her well.

'What is it, Aunt?' Giles finally asked her, having watched as she picked at her food throughout the meal but ate nothing.

Emily's hand shook momentarily as she poured their coffee, although she soon regained her equilibrium. 'Wrong?' she asked lightly. 'What could possibly be wrong?'

'You tell me.' He was sitting beside Leonie on the sofa, his long legs stretched out in front of him.

'There's nothing wrong, my dear boy. If I seem a little preoccupied it's because I'm so excited about the plans for the wedding.'

'It isn't excitement,' Giles insisted. 'You're worried. Now tell us what's bothering you.'

'Noth—All right,' she sighed. 'I—er—I had a telephone call from Dawn this afternoon.'

'Hell!' Giles stood forcefully to his feet, pacing the room.

Leonie had seen him angry before, more times than she could mention, but never like this. Whoever this Dawn was she meant something in Giles' life. A shaft of jealousy racked Leonie's body.

'What did she want?' he demanded, his face a mask of anger.

Emily was even more agitated. 'She's come back to England to attend the wedding.'

'She isn't coming!' Giles instantly denied. 'I don't want her at my wedding. How did she know about it?' he asked suspiciously.

'I—er—I——' Emily bit her lip in a distracted fashion. 'I told her, Giles. I thought she should know.'

'You should have asked me first,' he snapped. 'She has no right to know anything about my life, no right at all.'

'But, Giles——'

'She isn't coming here, is she?' he cut in.

Emily nodded. 'Tomorrow.'

'What time?' he asked grimly.

'In the morning some time. I thought she could stay to lunch——'

'I'll be out,' Giles told her curtly. 'And so will Leonie. And she'd better be gone before we get back.'

'Oh, Giles!'

'I mean it, Aunt. I will not see her.'

'Very well.' Emily stood up. 'I think I'll go to my room. I—I don't feel well.'

Leonie watched her go, wishing she could do something to take that bewildered hurt out of the older woman's eyes. 'What on earth is the matter with you?' she demanded of Giles once they were alone. 'Why did you talk to her like that?'

'Because I will not tolerate interference in my life, not even from my aunt.'

'Is it that important that you don't see this Dawn?' She frowned her puzzlement.

His eyes were like chips of ice. 'It isn't a question of importance,' he said furiously. 'I just won't see her.'

'But what's she done?'

'She's the ultimate betrayer,' he snapped. 'She walked out of my life once and I've made it a point never to readmit her. I don't want to see her, I don't want to have anything to do with her.'

'You love her,' Leonie said dully. He could only feel such vehemence towards the other woman if he loved her. She had hurt him, and even though she obviously regretted it Giles still refused to forgive her. While Leonie had believed him never to have loved anyone she had held out some hope of maybe having him fall in love with her in time. But now that she knew about Dawn that didn't even seem a remote possibility.

'I do not love her,' he denied savagely—too savagely.

'You must do. How else could you talk to Emily that way? You've hurt her dreadfully.'

He sighed. 'That can't be helped. She knew better than to interfere in this matter.'

'You're a despot!' Leonie's eyes blazed. 'You rule everyone's life like some feudal overlord.' She pulled the ring off her finger. 'Well, I won't be ruled any more.' She put the ring down on the table. 'Go and find someone else to bully!' and she marched over to the door.

'Where are you going?' Giles questioned softly.

She turned to see the ring held in the palm of his hand. She blinked back the tears. 'I'm going to be with the people who love me.'

'No!' his cry was pained. 'You can't leave me now.'

'Why can't I?' Her chin was held high.

'Because you're going to marry me!'

'You need my agreement for that. And I no longer agree! It was quite fun while it lasted.' She made her tone sound light. 'I'm sure Phil and I will have a good laugh over it.'

'Phil?' His eyes narrowed. 'You're going to Trent?'

She shrugged. 'Or Jeremy. Oh yes,' she insisted at his cry of protest, 'he still wants me. You didn't really believe that story about an old aunt, did you, Giles?' she scorned. 'Jeremy still has the flat, you know. Of course——' she broke off as his hand struck her cheeks.

'You little bitch!' he snarled. 'You promiscuous little bitch! All right, go to him. Go on, get out!'

'I intend to.' She held her throbbing cheek, knowing that things were finally over between Giles and herself. Being with Jeremy four years ago was one thing, going to him now was something else. But knowing Giles loved this Dawn ... She couldn't hold out hope for something that would never happen when he loved another woman. 'I never intended marrying you anyway,' she told him harshly. 'When you made that announcement I toyed with the idea of turning you down in front of your friends. But then I decided that this way it would get much more publicity—after all, the whole country knows of our engagement now. It was even worth putting up with your insulting behaviour just to have the pleasure of giving you back your ring now.'

'So you got your revenge after all.' His fingers clamped about the ring. 'My God, how you must be enjoying this!'

She wasn't enjoying anything, she was numb. She

was saying all the right things to alienate him for ever, and yet she didn't know how she was doing it when her heart was breaking.

'It's been quite fun,' she said lightly. 'Of course the cheque will be returned to you. Phil didn't cash it because he isn't stupid enough to give you leverage to charge him with anything, but it was interesting to see how far you would go.'

'Get out of here!' He turned his back on her. 'I don't ever want to see you again.'

'Don't worry, you won't,' she told him with conviction.

CHAPTER NINE

LEONIE didn't go straight to Phil that night, she went to a hotel instead. She needed time to think, to sort out her thoughts. The only trouble was the time at the hotel didn't do that, she was more confused than ever. She had blown any chance of ever being able to marry Giles now, and yet knowing he loved Dawn she had known she couldn't be his wife.

Phil opened her knock on the door, his anxious expression giving way to relief when he saw who it was. 'Leonie! Thank God,' he sighed, running a weary hand over his eyes.

'What's wrong?' she frowned. 'Nothing's happened to Wanda, has it?' She couldn't think of any other reason for him to be in this state. His clothes looked as if he had slept in them, although on closer inspection he didn't look as if he had slept at all; his eyes were bloodshot.

'No, of course it hasn't.' He pulled her roughly inside and closed the door. 'Where the hell have you been?'

'Where have I——? What do you mean?'

'I mean where were you all last night? I've been worried out of my mind.'

'But why? I mean, how did you know about—about——'

'About your broken engagement? About your leaving Rose Cottage?' he derided. 'How do you think I know?'

'Giles . . .?' she said disbelievingly.

'Who else?' Phil grimaced. 'And his mood wasn't pretty, Leonie.'

'But why did he get in touch with you? He told me to get out.'

'Maybe he did, but he wants to see you now. And he didn't just get in touch with me, Leonie,' he sighed. 'He turned up here at two o'clock in the morning. Thank God last night was one of the times Wanda decided to go back to her own flat.'

'Giles came *here*?' She couldn't understand it, not when he had told her to go.

Phil shrugged. 'He seemed to think this was where you would be. When I said you weren't he muttered something about Jeremy Lindsay. What does he have to do with this? Noble made it sound as if you were seeing him again.'

'Yes, well, I—We've met.'

'Noble made it sound more than that.'

'Then he was wrong. Look, Phil, I'm sorry he disturbed you, I didn't want you involved in this any more, but I don't want any more to do with Giles. We're finished—if we ever got started.'

'Finally came to your senses, did you?'

'Something like that,' she nodded.

'Well, Noble hasn't come to his. This bed-sitter may not be very big, but he searched every square inch of it. He said something about going to Lindsay's flat. What's going on, Leonie?'

She sank down on to the sofa. 'It's too complicated to explain. All right,' she sighed at his protest. 'I'll tell you.'

'At least you're off Lindsay's hook,' said Phil when she had finished.

'Mm. But I wonder why Giles decided to come after me,' she said thoughtfully.

'I have no idea. But——' he broke off as a knock sounded on the door. 'I think you may be going to find out.'

Leonie's expression was one of horror. 'You don't think that's him?'

'What do you think?' he asked dryly, moving to the door.

'Don't answer it, Phil,' she pleaded. 'I—I'm not up to another session of his insults.'

'I won't let him insult you, Leonie. Don't worry.'

But when he opened the door it was to reveal Wanda. 'Hi,' she kissed him soundly on the lips. 'I left my key here yesterday. Leonie!' She smiled her pleasure and moved to kiss her on the cheek. 'How lovely to see you!' She turned to Phil. 'My God, darling you look a wash-out!'

'I feel it,' he grimaced.

Wanda put her shoulder-bag on the floor. 'Well, here's something to cheer you both up.' She giggled delightedly. 'Someone gave my dear Daddy a black eye last night.' She chuckled. 'You should see him—it's come up all purple and black, with a lovely shade of constrasting yellow.'

Leonie swallowed hard. 'Somebody hit him?'

'Mm,' Wanda nodded, smiling happily. 'I think some jealous husband has finally caught him out. I went round this morning, on my usual monthly visit, and Daddy was sitting there with this beauty of a black eye,' she burst out laughing. 'Oh, he was furious!'

Leonie was very pale. 'Did he say who hit him?'

'No. By the time I had finished laughing at him he'd walked out of the room in a huff. Mummy isn't speaking to him, but I don't think she did it. She's probably just annoyed that he got found out.'

'But she didn't say who'd hit him either?' Phil probed softly.

'No,' Wanda was beginning to frown, noticing their serious expressions.

Leonie looked at her brother. 'Phil, you don't think . . .?'

'It has to be,' he confirmed her unvoiced thoughts. 'He said he was going round there.'

'Yes, but . . .' She shook her head. 'Surely he wouldn't——'

'You didn't see the mood he was in. If Jeremy Lindsay got away with a black eye then he was lucky.'

Comprehension seemed to dawn on Glenda, and she gasped. 'You don't mean——? Not Giles? Are you saying that Giles beat Daddy up?' She was incredulous.

'I think so,' Phil nodded.

'Wow!' she breathed softly.

'But why?' Leonie cried. 'Why is he doing this?'

'I think you would have to ask him that,' Phil told her. 'He's too complex a man for me to even begin to work out.'

She stood up. 'Well, I'm not staying here, not when he could come back here at any moment. And if he does come looking for me you aren't to tell him where I am.'

'Leonie——'

'I mean it, Phil. Now that I've made the break I don't want to see him again. He exerts a magnetism over me that I just can't resist,' she admitted reluctantly. 'So I want you to keep quiet about where I am.'

'What I was trying to say,' Phil smiled, 'is that I don't know *where* you are.'

She looked startled, then she returned his smile. 'No, you don't, do you? Then I won't tell you, then you won't have to lie if Giles does happen to ask.'

'Happen to ask!' her brother repeated scornfully. 'He's likely to beat *me* up if I don't tell him.'

'But you don't know,' she told him happily. 'So you'll be okay.'

'Leonie!' He stopped her exit. 'I think I should know where you are. I promise I won't tell Noble, no matter what pressure he exerts, but I don't like to think of you just disappearing like this. Besides, we need to contact you for the wedding. You'll come now, won't you?'

'Oh, please do, Leonie,' Wanda cut in pleadingly. 'You'll be the only family we have.'

Leonie bit her lip. 'When is it?'

'Wednesday. Well, we didn't see any point in waiting,' Phil explained at her surprised glance. 'At least this way we'll be able to save on one rent.'

'I just love that romantic streak in him,' Wanda teased.

'By the way, Leonie,' Phil spoke again, 'I gave Noble his cheque back. I didn't want the damned thing in the first place.'

'No,' she accepted, 'I didn't think you would. You see, Giles makes me do things, say things I wouldn't normally dream of doing. He seems to expect the worst of me and so that's what I give him. But I'm not really like that, and last night I realised I could no longer play the part he'd given me. But I played the bitch to the end,' she recalled bitterly. 'That's what he called me, a promiscuous little bitch.'

'And you still as innocent as a baby!' Phil snorted.

She sighed. 'Giles would never believe that. Okay, I'll meet you here on Wednesday. What time?'

'The wedding is at twelve, so I should get here about eleven-thirty, Phil advised.

She had to get in touch with Simon Watts next, Emily's publisher, and let him know she had broken her contract. He seemed to be expecting her, as his secretary ushered her straight into his office.

Simon's office had to be seen to be believed. There were books everywhere, on the floor, on the chairs, but most of all on the desk. Simon looked the part of the typical absentminded professor, his suit creased, his tie slightly askew, his rimless glasses perched on the end of his nose, something they insisted on doing even though he was constantly pushing them back into place.

'Leonie, my dear,' he quickly moved to clear a chair for her, 'how lovely to see you!'

'Emily and I were here only last week, Simon,' she reminded him. They had called to discuss the progress of the book with him, and Emily had persuaded him to take them out to lunch. It took a lot to drag Simon away from his books, he lived, ate, and breathed them, and it was perhaps as well that he had remained a bachelor. No woman would ever put up with his total absorption in books.

'Were you?' he blinked. 'Oh yes, so you were.' He peered at her over the top of a huge pile of books. 'Well, what can I do for you?' he beamed at her.

'I've broken my contract,' she came straight to the point. 'I'm no longer living at Rose Cottage.'

He nodded. 'So Emily told me. Some lovers' tiff with her nephew, wasn't it?'

Leonie gasped. She would hardly call a broken engagement a *lovers' tiff*. Besides, they weren't lovers, if they had been they may not have argued. 'Has Emily been in touch with you today?' she frowned.

Simon nodded. 'First thing this morning. I was hardly in the office when her call came in. Her nephew has been here too.'

'Giles has been *here?*' Her eyes were wide.

'Mm. He seems a nice young man, very worried about you.'

'About me?' Her frown deepened. What on earth was wrong with Giles? Why was he looking for her like this?

'Well, of course, my dear. The poor man has been up all night searching for you. Don't you think you should call him and let him know you're all right?'

'Simon——'

'I know, I know, it's none of my business. But he did look so worried.'

'For Emily's sake,' she said firmly, determined not to get into a discussion about Giles and herself, 'what did she have to say about the illustrations? Does she want to get someone else to do it?'

'No, no, my dear,' he smiled his vague smile. 'She doesn't want to do that. The illustrations are going so well, and the book's nearly finished. No, Emily is quite prepared for you to carry on.'

'But—but how?' Her relief was immense, her enjoyment in her work the one thing that didn't seem to have changed the last few weeks. 'I mean——'

'Through me,' Simon supplied. 'Emily will send her requirements through me to you—until such time as you patch up this argument with Mr Noble and move back to the cottage.'

'It isn't just an argument, Simon. Giles and I aren't getting married now. But I'm more than willing to finish this book with Emily.'

'Right.' Somehow Simon managed to find a blank piece of paper and a pen. 'If I could have your address . . .?'

Leonie flushed, sensing a trap. For some reason only he knew Giles wanted to see her, and he wasn't above tricking her into giving her whereabouts. She stood up. 'As you said, Simon, we'll keep in touch through you. I'll call again in a couple of days. I have enough to keep me going until then. I'll be in on Thursday, Simon. See you.'

What was Giles up to? She had started to wonder if perhaps there was something wrong with Emily, and that was why he was trying to contact her, but that was now ruled out. She couldn't even begin to think what he wanted to see her for, just as she couldn't imagine why he had hit Jeremy.

Wednesday dawned bright and sunny, an ideal day for a wedding. Leonie donned a deep blue silky dress and, attached a white rose to her breast.

Phil was in a terrible flap when she arrived at his bed-sitter. 'Thank God you're here!' he groaned. 'I just don't know what to do.'

'What is it?' Leonie sat down. 'Does your shirt need ironing or something?' she teased, eyeing his bathrobe-clad body questioningly.

'Much worse than that—Wanda's father has insisted on coming to the wedding!'

Leonie stiffened. 'Jeremy has?' she asked tightly.

'Yes.' Phil ran a hand through his already tousled hair. 'Wanda told him she was getting married. Now somehow he's found out where and says he's going to be there.'

She turned away. 'Will Wanda's mother be there too?'

'No,' he sighed. 'Apparently she's annoyed because Wanda made the arrangements secretly. God, what a bloody mess! Do they still have that bit at a register office wedding where they ask if there's anyone object-ing to the marriage taking place? You know the bit I mean, "Is there any just cause why this man and woman should not be joined together"—that bit,' he grimaced.

'I don't know, I suppose so.' She shook her head. 'You don't think he would——? Oh, surely not!'

'Oh, surely yes. I'm not a very good risk as a son-in-law, now am I? He'll stop the wedding, and by the time it's been sorted out that he has no right to stop it everything will be ruined.'

'Not necessarily.' She thought quickly. 'I think I may have a way of stopping him.'

'Leonie . . .' he looked uncertain, 'I don't want you doing anything you'll regret later. It isn't worth that.'

She gave a light laugh. 'I promise not to do anything stupid. I'll just divert him a little. Does he know you're the bridegroom?'

'Wanda refused to tell him who she was marrying.'

'Brave girl! Okay, you get ready. Just leave Jeremy to me.' She sounded very assured, but she wasn't at all sure she could handle Jeremy. After all, Wanda was his only child, and it was only to be expected that he would want the best for her. The fact that Phil was the best, except for one slip, would escape Jeremy, she felt sure of that.

'You were right the first time,' Phil grimaced. 'My shirt isn't ironed. Wanda moved out a couple of days ago, for propriety's sake, and I suppose I've got used to her doing those things for me. The last lot of laundry I brought back is still in the plastic bag.'

She found it in the corner. 'What colour is your suit?'

'Blue.'

By the time Phil had finally got himself ready it was almost twelve, then the taxi was delayed in heavy traffic.

'Calm down,' Leonie teased. 'I'm sure Wanda will wait for you.'

'But the registrar might not.'

'We're almost there.' She held his hand.

It seemed to be absolute chaos once they stepped out of the taxi. Wanda was white-faced, a furious Jeremy at her side.

'You aren't marrying my daughter,' he snarled at Phil.

'Daddy——'

'Stay out of this, Wanda. I should have realised when you wouldn't talk about him that you had something to hide!'

'Now listen here, Lindsay,' Phil was obviously furious over Wanda's distressed state.

'No, *you* listen. My daughter is not marrying you!'

'Jeremy——'

'And you can be quiet,' he turned on Leonie. 'You knew about this all the time.'

'Leave her out of it,' Phil defended. 'She was as surprised as you are about Wanda and me.'

Leonie wasn't exactly listening to them any more, she was staring at the tall impressive man who had just entered the building. Giles! He seemed like an oasis in a desert in the midst of this mess. She hurried to his side.

He looked just as smart as always, the navy blue suit and lighter coloured shirt fitting him as immaculately as usual. And yet there it ended; Giles was haggard. His grey eyes were sunken into their sockets, his face drawn and pale, his movements jerky and disjointed.

His expression lightened as he saw her. 'Leonie . . .' he choked. 'Oh God, Leonie!' He closed his eyes as if not quite believing she was real.

'Giles, I need your help.' Right now Phil and

Wanda's happiness was uppermost in her mind, and if anyone could bring calm to this situation then Giles could. 'Could you——'

'We have to talk, Leonie,' he grasped her arm. 'Let's go somewhere more private.'

'I can't,' she refused. 'Giles, Jeremy is making a scene about the wedding.'

He seemed to become aware of the other three for the first time. 'What do you want me to do?' He looked down at her.

'Get him out of here, any way you can. Oh, look, the registrar is calling them in now,' she was agitated. The wedding obviously couldn't take place with Jeremy still here.

'Leonie, will you talk to me, afterwards?'

'I—I—Yes. Just get him away from here,' she said desperately.

'Leonie——'

'Please, Giles,' she looked up at him pleadingly. 'I promise you we'll talk later.'

'I've been looking for you for days,' he groaned, his eyes agonised.

'I know,' she answered absently, aware that the registrar was becoming impatient.

Giles followed her line of vision. 'Okay,' he sighed, 'I'll deal with Jeremy.'

'And peacefully,' she put in hurriedly. 'Don't get violent here!'

'You heard about that,' he smiled ruefully.

'Yes. Wanda thought it was hilarious.' And she had to admit to a certain amount of enjoyment herself when she had seen the yellowy-purple eye a few minutes ago.

Giles quirked one dark eyebrow. 'Not interested in the reasoning behind it?'

'Not at this moment, no. If they don't go in soon the whole thing will have to be cancelled.'

She watched in admiration as he strode over to the other group and instantly took charge. He told the registrar the bride and groom would be in with him in two minutes, and the little man scuttled back into his office.

'I might have known you had a hand in this!' Jeremy turned on him viciously. 'You and Leonie both!'

'I've warned you once this week about being insulting to Leonie,' Giles told him icily. 'I would be quite willing to enforce that lesson once again.'

Jeremy paled at the threat in the other man's voice. 'That won't be necessary.'

'I thought not,' Giles drawled, looking pointedly at the discoloured eye. 'Now shall we both walk quietly out of here or do you want me to use force?'

Jeremy flushed his resentment. 'Wanda is my daughter——'

'Is she?' Giles cut in tautly. 'There's more to being a father than being the man who helped conceive her, and as far as I can see you've done little else for Wanda. Whereas Phil—well, he's made her happy.'

'He has no means of supporting her!'

'I don't need supporting,' Wanda snapped resentfully.

'No, she doesn't,' Giles agreed. 'She and Phil are going to work together, both in marriage and business.'

'I don't understand——'

'It's quite simple, Jeremy. Leonie and I are going to help them open a restaurant.'

'Giles!' Leonie gasped.

'Take Phil and Wanda in, Leonie,' he advised huskily, turning to Phil. 'I'm afraid you'll have to get someone else to be your other witness. I'm going to be otherwise occupied,' he drawled.

'Wanda——'

'I'm sorry, Daddy. It's Phil I love, and I'm going to marry him.'

'Let's go, Jeremy,' Giles said tautly.

'But——'

'Mr Trent!' The registrar appeared in the doorway. 'Mr Trent, we have to perform the ceremony now or I'm afraid you'll have to come back another time.'

'We're coming now,' Wanda assured him. 'Goodbye, Daddy,' and she and Phil entered the inner office.

Leonie felt sorry for Jeremy in that moment, although the glare he directed at her showed he didn't want or need her pity.

'I'll see you in hell for this!' he rasped.

'You could see us in court first,' Giles snapped, his hand firmly grasping Leonie's elbow. 'If you ever dare to threaten Leonie again,' he added tautly.

The eyes Jeremy turned on her were vehement. 'You told him about that!' he accused. 'You little——'

'Leonie didn't tell me anything,' Giles interrupted harshly. 'She wouldn't. My information came from a different source.'

'That damned brother of hers, I suppose,' Jeremy scowled.

'Not him either.'

'Leonie!' An exasperated-looking Phil appeared in the doorway. 'We've been given exactly one minute to get our wedding party together.'

She nodded. 'I'm coming now.'

'We both are,' Giles drawled. 'I can trust you to leave of your own accord, can't I, Jeremy?'

'I'll be glad to!' He stormed out.

Leonie looked up at Giles with dazed eyes, unable

not to think of the enigmatic statements he had been making this afternoon. Apparently Phil had invited him to be the other witness to the wedding, and there had also been some mention of Giles and Phil going into business together with the restaurant. And yet she was sure Phil had given Giles his cheque back.

'Can we start now?' the registrar asked disapprovingly once they had all taken their places.

'I believe you can go ahead,' Giles nodded, his amusement barely contained as he caught Leonie's glance.

Despite its chaotic start, and her puzzlement over Giles, she found the wedding very moving. Wanda looked starry-eyed, and Phil looked sheepishly proud, and in no time they were husband and wife.

'Lunch is on me,' said Giles once they emerged out into the sunshine.

'No,' Phil insisted firmly, 'lunch is on me.'

'Fine,' Giles accepted. 'Shall we go in my car?'

Phil grinned. 'I was hoping you'd offer, I fancy a ride in a Rolls!'

Leonie went along with this, feeling that the day had been disaster enough already. But she had no wish to spend time with Giles, sitting quietly as the other three chatted together over the meal in the quiet Italian restaurant Phil and Wanda chose.

'Nice place.' Giles sat back, his brandy in a glass in front of him. 'Anything like the place you want to set up?' he asked Phil.

'How did you guess?' Phil grinned. 'Very similar, only the cuisine will be English.'

Giles nodded. 'Very wise. The quietly exclusive restaurant is coming back into fashion.'

'You really think it could work?' Wanda asked eagerly.

'Of course, as long as you attract the right clientele from the beginning. As I was telling Phil the other evening, I'll probably be able to help you out with that.'

'Of course you will,' Wanda laughed. 'You know all those rich barristers.'

Giles smiled. 'They aren't all rich.'

'The other evening?' Leonie couldn't maintain her silence any longer, determined to get to the bottom of this conversation.

Her brother flushed. 'Giles—er—Mr Noble and I——'

'Giles,' he corrected smoothly.

Phil nodded. 'Giles has offered to go into business with me,' he told Leonie.

'And he did this the other night,' she said dryly.

'Yes.' Phil stared down at his empty coffee cup.

'When the two of you, who have always professed to dislike each other, got into a cosy little chat about the restaurant business, such a cosy little chat that Giles even offered to finance your venture,' her voice was shrill. 'In fact you became such good friends over this *cosy little chat* that you even asked him to attend your wedding as the second witness.'

'Leonie——'

'Well, forgive me for being surprised,' she cut in tautly. 'But the last I heard you couldn't stand each other.' Her eyes flashed deeply blue in her agitation. 'Now you're going to be business partners.'

'I think we can discuss this when we're alone, Leonie,' Giles told her firmly. 'Phil and Wanda's wedding day has been traumatic enough already, without our adding to it.'

Wanda cuddled up to Phil. 'As long as we're married nothing else matters.'

She received a kiss from her husband for that. 'I think it's better if we have this thing out in the open,' he said tolerantly, turning to Leonie. 'Giles and I had this "cosy little chat" because of you——'

'*Me?* You have no need——'

'Because he's been out of his mind with worry about you,' Phil continued in a firm voice. 'So have I, for that matter. I didn't expect you to just disappear until this morning. You could have let me know how you were.'

'I'm sorry,' her sarcasm was unmistakable. She felt slightly hysterical, as if the whole world were ganging up on her. Phil and Giles now seemed to be firm friends, had become so because of a mutual worry about *her*. 'I didn't realise I had to report back to anyone on my movements,' she continued. 'I thought all that had stopped when I gave Giles back his ring.'

'I really do think it would be better if Leonie and I discussed this somewhere else.' Giles' mouth was taut. 'Perferably somewhere we can be alone.'

'I don't want to be alone with you,' she snapped. 'Why don't you go and be alone with—with Sonja, or—or Dawn?' she added in a rush.

'Dawn . . .?' he frowned his puzzlement. 'What does she have to do with us?'

'Everything,' she told him furiously. 'I witnessed your reaction to Emily getting in touch with her, don't forget. And if one of your ex-girl-friends can make you react like that then I just don't want to know.'

'Girl-friend?' He sounded astounded. 'Dawn?'

'Don't act so innocent. You were very rude about her. And you upset Emily terribly.'

'I should think I damn well did!'

'Calm down, Giles,' Phil chuckled. 'I think maybe you're right, and you should take Leonie away from here, somewhere you can kiss some sense into her. She sounds like a jealous female to me.'

'Phil!' She flushed, wondering just what he had told Giles the other evening. Not that she loved him, surely! 'Be quiet!' she snapped. 'Just because you've had this sudden change of feeling towards Giles it doesn't mean we all have,' her look was a warning.

'It's obvious you haven't,' Giles said tightly, setting her mind at rest about Phil having revealed her secret love for him. 'But I think it's time Phil and Wanda went off on their honeymoon. Leonie and I can sort out our own difficulties once you've gone.'

Leonie looked startled. 'You're going away?' she asked her brother.

'Just for a few days.' He looked uncomfortable, adding nothing to the statement.

'Where have they gone?' she demanded of Giles once they had dropped the other couple off at the station.

'To my cottage in Wales,' he answered easily, driving the Rolls with controlled speed through the busy London streets.

'I should have known,' she scoffed. 'You've taken over their lives as easily as you took over mine. You won't get me back this way, Giles, not through bribery.'

'My business deal with Phil has nothing to do with you,' he told her in a stilted voice.

'I realise you're piqued because you didn't get me into bed with you, but——'

'Shut up!'

'I will not!' She glared at him. 'Helping my brother out doesn't mean I feel any more kindly disposed towards you.'

He ran a weary hand through his grey-speckled dark

hair. 'You've already made your feelings towards me more than clear.'

'Then why have you been looking for me? Why can't you just leave me alone?'

'After today I will,' he assured her.

'Where are you taking me?' she wanted to know, seeing the purpose in his expression.

'To my house. There's someone there I want you to meet.'

'Not Emily,' she denied with a groan. 'I can't see her just now, I'm too embarrassed. Maybe in a few weeks' time.'

'It isn't Emily, she's still at the cottage.'

Leonie frowned. 'Then who is it?'

'Wait and see,' came his noncommittal answer.

She couldn't get any more information out of him, his mood was so adamant, so she had to be content to sit and seethe as they drove to his house.

Davenport let then in when they arrived, not seeming at all surprised by Leonie's presence, although he surely must have heard of their broken engagement.

'Is Mrs Burroughs here?' Giles asked him.

'She's been out since this morning, sir, but she did say she would be back early this afternoon.'

'Very well,' Giles nodded. 'Mrs Carter and I will be waiting in the lounge when she returns.'

Leonie followed him with ill-grace, hating being manoeuvred like this. 'Who is Mrs Burroughs?' she wanted to know.

'Drink?' He moved to the drinks trolley, ignoring her question.

'No—thank you.' She watched as he poured himself one. 'Are you still drinking too much?'

'Yes!' the explosion was savage.

Leonie bit her lip. 'This Mrs Burroughs, who is she?' she persisted.

He took a swallow of the whisky. 'If I tell you her first name is Dawn will that help you?' his tone was scornful.

'Dawn?' she echoed sharply. 'You actually have her living here with you?'

'Yes. Leonie, she——' he broke off as the sound of voices could be heard out in the hallway. 'That must be her now.'

Leonie was furious. 'I'm not staying!'

His eyes were narrowed to icy slits. 'You'll meet her.'

'No——'

The door swung open and a woman walked in. 'Ah, Giles,' she moved to kiss him on the cheek. 'And you've brought your fiancée to meet me at last,' she smiled warmly at Leonie.

'Mother,' Giles greeted tersely.

Mother! Leonie looked at them dazedly. For not only was Dawn Burroughs Giles' mother, she was also the woman who had been staring so intently at Jeremy and herself when they had had lunch together at the Ritz!

CHAPTER TEN

THE woman gave a light laugh. 'Don't look so surprised, Leonie—I may call you Leonie, I hope?' she smiled at Leonie's nod of assent. 'I am indeed Giles' mother.'

'But I—I didn't know,' Leonie flushed. 'What I mean is——'

'You mean you thought I was dead,' Giles' mother finished easily. 'That's the way he prefers to think of me, don't you, dear?'

'Mother,' he said warningly.

'Well, it's true,' she told him happily. 'I know that. And until the last few years I might just as well have been. I'm perfectly well aware of the fact that I've been a lousy mother.'

'Leonie isn't interested in this,' Giles said tautly.

'Yes, I am,' she denied abruptly. 'I'm very interested in your mother. It's so nice to meet you, Mrs Burroughs, it proves that Giles is human after all. I'd begun to think he was simply carved out of granite.' She knew by his furious expression that she had hit a sensitive spot—as she had intended to.

Mrs Burroughs obviously appreciated the remark, though. She openly joined in Leonie's amusement. 'How long did you say the two of you have known each other?' she asked her son.

'Four years,' he revealed tightly.

She shook her head. 'And you haven't once proved that you're human, in all that time?'

Now it was Giles' turn to smile. 'Oh, I think I've

done that—on occasion.'

Leonie blushed. 'But he soon reverts to type,' she snapped. 'I don't know whether you're aware of the fact, Mrs Burroughs, but your son is a very suspicious individual.'

The other woman quirked her eyebrows. 'Maybe he has reason for that sometimes, hmm?'

Leonie knew the the occasion to which she alluded. 'Maybe,' she admitted curtly. 'Although things aren't always what they seem.'

'I know that, dear,' she said gently. 'That's why I had to tell Giles about your seeing Jeremy Lindsay. Not that I knew who he was at the time, but Giles was able to recognise him by my description of him.'

Leonie's eyes were wide as she turned to look at Giles. 'You know why I saw Jeremy?'

'Not until my mother turned up.'

'I'm sorry, Leonie,' Mrs Burroughs spoke to her, 'but I didn't like that man's tone at all.'

'You were Giles' other source . . .' she said dazedly. 'I was?'

'Yes. You see——'

'You should have told me, Leonie,' Giles interrupted angrily, 'instead of letting me jump to conclusions.'

'Conclusions you were only too happy to jump to,' she accused.

'All right,' he sighed. 'I'll admit to doing that a lot where you're concerned, but you've never tried to help matters.'

'*Help* them?' she scorned. 'You didn't believe me when I did tell the truth. You enjoy thinking the worst of me, you always have.'

'No,' he said intently. 'Leonie, I——'

'It isn't going to work, Giles,' she told him angrily.

'Not even to save your mother embarrassment will I——'

'Oh, I'm not embarrassed, Leonie,' Mrs Burroughs smiled her pleasure. 'It's a change to see Giles not getting his own way.'

'Mother!'

'You don't frighten me, Giles,' she smiled. 'And you don't intimidate Leonie either. She seems perfectly capable of standing up for herself.' she said happily.

'She is,' Giles admitted grimly. 'So perhaps you wouldn't mind leaving us so that she can do exactly that.'

She raised her eyebrows at Leonie. 'Not very tactful, is he?'

'Or polite,' Leonie agreed with a glare in his direction.

'How the hell can I be polite when you're driving me quietly out of my mind?' he rasped.

'Giles!' She looked pointedly at his mother.

'Oh, don't mind me, dear,' Mrs Burroughs said happily.

'But *I* do,' Giles said grimly. 'Would you mind leaving Leonie and me alone?'

She stood up with a certain amount of reluctance. 'Just as the conversation was getting interesting too!'

'I'm sure it was,' he said grimly.

'If you take my advice, Giles—which you never have,' she added without rancour, 'then you'll marry this perfectly charming young lady.'

He raised his eyebrows. 'And if she won't have me?'

'I've never known you to be negative, Giles,' his mother chided. 'Make her marry you.'

'That's what I've been trying to do,' he sighed. 'And with Leonie that method doesn't work.'

'It might have done,' Leonie told him vehemently,

'if you hadn't been cruel and sadistic too.'

'Giles!' his mother cried in dismay. 'What have you been doing to this child?'

His expression darkened. 'Trying to show her that she belongs to me,' he said fiercely.

His mother tutted. 'That's where you've been going wrong. Really, Giles, I'm surprised at you! I would have thought you knew women better than this. Stake a claim on a woman and she'll fight you to hell and back.'

Giles grimaced. 'Your terminology leaves a lot to be desired.'

His mother gave him an impatient look. 'What does it matter, as long as my meaning is clear? The way to get a woman to marry you is to tell her you love her, not tell her she *belongs* to you.' His mother left the room with a quiet click of the door.

'Whew!' Leonie breathed. 'Now I know who you get it from.'

Giles's mouth was tight. 'You believe I'm like my mother?'

'Exactly like her,' she nodded. 'If only she realised you don't know how to love, that you were only marrying me at all because you couldn't possess me any other way.'

He moved to pour himself a drink, swallowing the whisky in one gulp. 'Couldn't I?' he said tautly.

'No!' Colour flamed her cheeks.

Giles breathed deeply. '*Yes*, Leonie. And that wasn't the reason at all. I didn't want to marry you for any other reason than that I—I love you.' He put a hand up over his eyes. 'I love you so much that I can't live without you. Why do you think I've been acting like a madman, why I came after you even though you said you'd been with Jeremy?'

Leonie had gone very white, wishing he would take his hand away so that she could see his face. 'Giles . . .?' she said disbelievingly.

His hand snapped back, his face haggard. 'Yes, laugh if you want to, I think I deserve that.'

She swallowed hard, her gaze fixed on his haggard features. He wasn't being sarcastic, or cruel, or any of the things he had been the last few weeks, he was being completely honest. Giles *loved* her! 'I—I'm not laughing,' her voice faltered. 'I think I may be going mad, but I'm not laughing. Giles, do you mean what you're saying?'

'That I love you?' he rasped harshly. 'Of course.'

'But—but how?'

His mouth twisted into a self-derisory smile. 'Most women ask when, not how.'

'All right,' she quavered. 'When?'

'As soon as I saw you in the courtroom four years ago,' he revealed dully.

'I don't believe that,' she shook her head. 'I don't care what game it is you're playing now,' she said angrily, 'but I'm not interested. I'd like to leave now.'

'No!' His cry was agonised. 'I won't let you go. You can't leave!'

'Watch me.' She spun on her heel.

'No, you can't go, Leonie!' He spun her round, deep grooves of tension beside his nose and mouth. 'I won't let you,' he choked, pulling her close against him. 'Don't leave me, Leonie. For God's sake don't go.' He trembled against her, his face buried in her throat.

He couldn't be playing, even he wasn't this good an actor. 'Giles, I—I don't know what to say.' Her arms went about his waist, her head resting against his shoulder. 'You—I—Tell me about it.'

'I love you,' he groaned. 'Whatever else, please believe that.'

'I'm trying,' she said huskily.

Giles drew a ragged breath, and put her firmly away from him. 'I can't think straight when I hold you, and I think if I was at least comprehensible when I talk to you it may help.'

She gave a jerky smile. 'It may do.'

'All right.' He ran an unsteady hand through his already tousled hair, his usual impeccable appearance noticeably absent. 'I'll start from the beginning. When Jeremy asked me to take his case I accepted because he was a friend. During the next few weeks I listened to him telling me what a devious, money-grasping little bitch you were. By the time of the trial I felt I knew you almost as well as he did. Then I saw you for myself ...' He shook his head. 'I'd never even believed in love, let alone love at first sight. And yet one look at you and I was lost.'

'You told me I should have been given life,' she recalled bitterly.

'Life with *me*. I wanted to marry you, tie you to me for a lifetime.'

'I hated you.'

'I know,' he sighed. 'Which was why I left you alone when the court case was over. By the time I decided you might be able to look at me without spitting in my face you'd moved from your flat, and you hadn't left a forwarding address. Shortly after that you must have got married, because I couldn't find you anywhere.'

Leonie frowned. 'Did you try?'

'God, yes. But I had to give up in the end. It just never occurred to me that you were married.'

She bit her bottom lip. 'Tell me, do you still believe what Jeremy told you about me?'

He shook his head. 'I don't think I ever did. Although it threw me a bit when you turned up at my aunt's and it looked as if the same thing was going to be tried on me.'

'I wasn't——'

'I tried not to believe it, but when I kissed you you responded. And considering that you hate me I considered that a suspicious reaction.'

Leonie looked down awkwardly at her hands. 'Maybe I just liked to be kissed by you.'

Hope kindled in his eyes 'Did you?'

'Go on,' she said hardly.

Giles sighed. 'Well, I liked kissing you anyway. I still do. As soon as I saw you again I knew I had to have you. Marry you,' he hastily explained as she frowned. 'Then you said that you had a price for letting me make love to you, and that that price was marriage. I rebelled against that, fought against being trapped into what I really wanted to do anyway. Then I thought I overheard you proposing to Phil!'

'He's my *brother*. He always has been.'

Giles nodded. 'So he explained. I like your brother, Leonie.'

'I think he likes you too,' she said dryly.

'I hope so. He made a mistake in his youth, but I think everyone is entitled to one mistake.'

'I wasn't!' she recalled indignantly.

'That was different, I'm in love with you. I don't allow any faults in the people I love. My mother——'

'Obviously hurt you very much. But that was years ago.'

He shrugged. 'It made a lasting impression. It made me even harder on the woman I finally fell in love with.'

'Me?'

'Yes.'

Leonie shook her head. 'I never stood a chance.'

'Not in the circumstances in which we met, no. But I fell in love with you anyway.'

'And made me suffer for it!'

'Yes,' he admitted heavily. 'But you didn't help. You did everything you could to make me think badly of you. When you asked for that money I could have wrung your neck.'

'You deserved that,' she said with feeling. 'You were high-handed and insulting—as usual.'

'But you still agreed to marry me.'

Her eyes sparkled angrily. 'You didn't give me any choice in the matter.'

'You know I did. You could have denied me in front of all my friends. But you didn't, and you continued to take my insults. Why was that, Leonie?' His piercing grey eyes probed her flushed and heated cheeks, her lashes lowering to shield her revealing eyes.

'Why, Leonie?' he repeated shakily.

'Because I—Maybe I thought you should suffer a while longer.'

'I've suffered, I'm still suffering.'

She could see that, could see the raw pain in his grey eyes, the tension about his mouth. She took a deep breath, deciding to tell him of her own love, of her own pain. 'Giles——'

'How could you still love Jeremy?' he suddenly exploded, banging his fist down on the table. 'How can you, after all that he's done to you?'

'But I——'

'God, I know *I'm* a swine, but at least I genuinely love you.'

'So does he, in his own way,' she said bitterly. 'He was going to divorce Glenda and marry me.'

Giles gave a defeated sigh. 'Then that's that. I—I hope you'll be happy with him.' He turned away.

Leonie couldn't stand it any more, wanted the nerve-shattering lovemaking that only Giles could give her. She put her hand on his arm, and felt him flinch. 'Do you really mean that?'

His expression was fierce as he looked down at her. 'I'll see him in hell first!' he snarled.

Her mouth twitched and then she began to laugh, at last beginning to believe in his love.

'What's so funny?' he growled.

'You are,' she smiled. 'I'm not going to marry Jeremy, Giles. I hope I never see him again.'

'Leonie——'

'I don't love him and I'm not marrying him,' she insisted firmly.

Giles frowned. 'But you do love him. I saw you the night of the dinner-party, saw your reaction to him.'

'Not him,' she contradicted softly, looking up at him with unflinching eyes, her hand moving up to caress his hard cheek. 'That night I looked at *you* and realised I love you.'

He swallowed hard. 'You—love—me?'

'Yes,' she gave a relieved laugh, 'I love you.'

'Really?'

'Yes, really,' she smiled.

His breath left his body in a hiss, his mouth turning to probe her palm as his gaze searched the glow of her face. 'Will you marry me?'

'Yes,' she agreed happily.

'Did you say—yes?'

'I did,' she nodded.

Giles eyes closed. 'I can't believe this. I've wanted—*loved* you for so long, I can't believe you'll really be my wife.'

'But I will. And when we're on our honeymoon you can tell me about how you and Phil became friends.'

The glimmer of a smile lightened his strained features. 'I think we might have things to do other than talk about your brother!'

Leonie blushed. 'I hope so.'

She woke to find the dawn just breaking over the roof-tops of Paris. And she was alone, only the warmth of the sheet next to her telling her that Giles had been beside her until a few minutes ago. Her husband of only a few hours!

She sat up, searching the gloom for him, seeing his silhouette against the window as daylight penetrated the room.

'Giles?' She frowned as he didn't answer. 'Giles, what's wrong?' She stood up, moving hurriedly to his side, unconcerned with her nakedness, feeling no shyness with the man who now knew her body more intimately than he knew his own, just as she knew every hard contour of his. 'Giles!' she cried her concern.

He looked down at her, the tears still wet on his cheeks. 'I didn't know,' he choked. 'I couldn't have known,' he groaned, burying his face into her scented throat.

She didn't even pretend not to know what he was talking about. Giles knew of her innocence now, knew her to be untouched by any man but him. 'I didn't know how to tell you,' she said softly.

'You mean you knew I wouldn't believe you even if you did tell me.' He was visibly shaking. 'Your husband . . .'

'Was an invalid. He married me for companionship, and I married him because—well, because he needed me and I loved him. Oh, not like I love you. Tom was a father figure. I liked and respected him very much. I—I think I made him happy.'

'And Jeremy told me nothing but lies!' Giles said savagely.

'It doesn't matter,' Leonie soothed him. 'Nothing else matters now that I'm your wife.'

'But the things I said to you, the accusations——'

'Are all in the past.' She pouted provocatively. 'It's very lonely in that big bed.'

'Leonie, how can you still want me?' he groaned with self-loathing.

She smiled confidently at him. 'It's quite simple, I can't *not* want you. Now, are you going to come back to bed with me?'

'Tonight and every other night.' His words were in the form of a vow.

PARIS—CITY OF ROMANCE

The very word "Paris" is like a magical incantation, conjuring up not just a city but a fairy-tale kingdom of romance and beauty. Parisians, proud of their home, assure everyone who will listen that "Paris is the most beautiful city in the world." A perfect spot for Giles and Leonie to honeymoon!

In the early morning a light mist rises off the River Seine and swirls against the gray stone walls of dozens of elaborately sculpted palaces: the Louvre, the Palais du Luxembourg, the Palais Royal, the Petit Palais and the Grand Palais. The list goes on, for Paris is a city of history and aristocracy.

From vantage points in the centers of hundreds of cobblestoned squares, with their towering monuments to heroes long dead or battles fought and won, visitors can watch the city come to life. The broad treelined avenues become crammed with cars; the sidewalks and cafés fill with pedestrians. A day may be spent browsing through the fabulous art collections at the Louvre, exploring the dark interiors of great cathedrals or climbing la tour Eiffel to gaze out over the roofs of the city.

As dusk falls the sidewalks cafés in the Latin quarter fill with elegantly dressed Parisians, perhaps discussing the evening ahead. For there is so much to do! First, perhaps, a gourmet dinner at Maxim's, or another of Paris's five-star restaurants. Then the Opéra, or the theater. And afterward, in the wee hours of the morning, there are the nightclubs of Pigalle: the Moulin Rouge, the Folies Bergéres, or the Concert Mayol.

But perhaps honeymooners like Giles and Leonie simply wish to go off by themselves, to walk along the Seine, which, like love, flows quietly and steadily through the exciting energy of the world's most beautiful city.

Harlequin Presents...

Take these
4 best-selling novels
FREE

That's right! FOUR first-rate Harlequin romance novels by four world renowned authors, FREE, as your introduction to the Harlequin Presents Subscription Plan. Be swept along by these FOUR exciting, poignant and sophisticated novels . . . . Travel to the Mediterranean island of Cyprus in **Anne Hampson**'s "Gates of Steel" . . . to Portugal for **Anne Mather**'s "Sweet Revenge" . . . to France and **Violet Winspear**'s "Devil in a Silver Room" . . . and the sprawling state of Texas for **Janet Dailey**'s "No Quarter Asked."

Join the millions of avid Harlequin readers all over the world who delight in the magic of a really exciting novel. EIGHT great NEW titles published EACH MONTH! Each month you will get to know exciting, interesting, true-to-life people . . . . You'll be swept to distant lands you've dreamed of visiting . . . . Intrigue, adventure, romance, and the destiny of many lives will thrill you through each Harlequin Presents novel.

 **The very finest in romantic fiction**

Get all the latest books before they're sold out!

As a Harlequin subscriber you actually receive your personal copies of the latest Presents novels immediately after they come off the press, so you're sure of getting all 8 each month.

Cancel your subscription whenever you wish!

You don't have to buy any minimum number of books. Whenever you decide to stop your subscription just let us know and we'll cancel all further shipments.

Your FREE gift includes

Sweet Revenge by **Anne Mather**
Devil in a Silver Room by **Violet Winspear**
Gates of Steel by **Anne Hampson**
No Quarter Asked by **Janet Dailey**

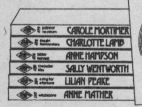